Praise f

"Engaging characters, ~~D0664202~~ and delight,
shivering suspense and captivating romance.
Want it all? Read Ann Major."
—Nora Roberts, *New York Times* bestselling author

"Ann Major delights readers
with memorable characters, sparkling dialogue
and tension that sizzles."
—bestselling author Mary Lynn Baxter

"Whenever I pick up a novel by Ann Major,
I know I'm guaranteed a heartwarming story."
—bestselling author Annette Broadrick

"No one provides hotter emotional fireworks
than the fiery Ann Major."
—*Romantic Times*

"Compelling characters, intense,
fast-moving plots and snappy dialogue have
made Ann Major's name synonymous with
the best in contemporary romantic fiction."
—*Rendezvous*

"Ann Major's SECRET CHILD sizzles
with characters who leap off the page
and into your heart… This one's hot!"
—bestselling author Lisa Jackson

Don't miss Signature Select's exciting series:

The Fortunes of Texas: Reunion

**Starting in June 2005, get swept up in
twelve new stories from your favorite family!**

THE FORTUNES OF TEXAS™
Reunion

COWBOY AT MIDNIGHT
Ann Major

Silhouette Books

Published by Silhouette Books
America's Publisher of Contemporary Romance

If you purchased this book without a cover you should be aware
that this book is stolen property. It was reported as "unsold and
destroyed" to the publisher, and neither the author nor the
publisher has received any payment for this "stripped book."

Special thanks and acknowledgment are given
to Ann Major for her contribution
to the FORTUNES OF TEXAS: REUNION series.

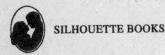

SILHOUETTE BOOKS

COWBOY AT MIDNIGHT

Copyright © 2005 by Harlequin Books S.A.

ISBN 0-373-38926-4

All rights reserved. Except for use in any review, the reproduction
or utilization of this work in whole or in part in any form by any
electronic, mechanical or other means, now known or hereafter
invented, including xerography, photocopying and recording, or in
any information storage or retrieval system, is forbidden without
the written permission of the editorial office, Silhouette Books,
233 Broadway, New York, NY 10279 U.S.A.

All characters in this book have no existence outside the imagination of
the author and have no relation whatsoever to anyone bearing the same
name or names. They are not even distantly inspired by any individual
known or unknown to the author, and all incidents are pure invention.

This edition published by arrangement with Harlequin Books S.A.

® and TM are trademarks of Harlequin Books S.A., used under license.
Trademarks indicated with ® are registered in the United States Patent
and Trademark Office, the Canadian Trade Marks Office and in other
countries.

Visit Silhouette Books at www.eHarlequin.com

Printed in U.S.A.

Dear Reader,

I hope you are well.

I had so much fun writing *Cowboy at Midnight*.

I think the most important skill a human being can have is the ability to grow and change and be flexible. We all start off in the Garden of Eden, or rather childhood, where life seems simple and sometimes miraculously wonderful—at least, if we are born into happy homes.

Then something happens, like a tragedy, that forces us to grow up too suddenly, and we see ourselves and our world in a brand-new light, sometimes a darker light. We can get stuck, not wanting to move on or accept ourselves as adults or forgive ourselves for not living up to some childish, untenable ideal.

Amy, my story's heroine, lost her dearest friend at an early age and blamed herself. She has punished herself for eight years.

Then she meets Steve, my hero, and falls in love. She can't let herself have him unless she changes.

I hope you enjoy THE FORTUNES OF TEXAS: REUNION.

Happy reading,

Ann Major

"We must have the courage
to allow a little disorder in our lives."
—Ben Weininger

I dedicate this book to Tara Gavin, Patience Smith,
Shannon Godwin, Karen Solem, Nancy Berland,
and Dianne Moggy—all brilliant women!
I owe you more than I can say! Thank you!

Prologue

Double Crown Ranch
Red Rock, Texas

*S*omebody was going to die!

Rosita Perez *knew* this as she threw off her sheets and cotton quilt and sprang out of bed.

The room felt as icy as a meat locker. Even so, her long black hair with its distinctive white streak above her forehead was soaking wet, as was her pillow. Hot flashes, her gringo doctor would say.

Smart gringo doctors thought they knew everything.

Rosita shuddered.

Somebody was going to die. Somebody close at hand.

She was descended from a long line of *curanderos*. Since birth she'd been cursed, or blessed, with the sight.

Like her ancestors, who'd been natural healers, she saw things. She felt things that other people didn't feel.

Life wasn't lived on a single plane. Nor was the world and its machinations entirely logical, much as her good-hearted bosses, Ryan and Lily Fortune, might like to think. She'd learned to keep her visions to herself because most people, including her beloved husband, Ruben, didn't believe her.

She'd had a strange nightmare that was both a riddle and a warning. In her dream a red moon had broken out of fierce, black whirling clouds and had hovered directly over the Double Crown Ranch. When she'd run outside and looked up, the red ball hadn't been the moon but a gigantic human skull floating above Lily and Ryan Fortune's ranch house. Rosita had awakened screaming to the skull, "No! Go away!"

Feeling too afraid to risk sleep again, she pulled on her robe and tiptoed out of the bedroom and down the dark hall, taking care not to wake Ruben. Just when she thought she'd made it, she crashed into her enormous bookcase in the hallway that was crammed with books and jars of herbs. Two books tumbled to the floor with loud thumps.

She prayed silently when she heard Ruben's snoring stop in midbreath. She barely breathed until he flopped his heavy, barrellike body onto his other side and resumed his snoring. Her house was too small, and all the rooms were cluttered, even the hall.

The bed groaned. Only when Ruben continued his roaring for a full minute did she tiptoe toward the front windows of her living room.

The ominous red glow that lit the window shades made her shake even more. Sensing evil, she felt her throat tighten every time she thought about going out on her front porch.

Which was ridiculous. She'd faced cougars and bobcats and convicts on the loose while living alone on ranches. Besides, Ruben was right down the hall.

Despite her misgivings, or maybe because of them, she opened the front door and forced herself to pad bravely out onto the porch of her small house.

The dense night smelled sweetly of juniper and buzzed with the music of millions of cicadas.

Summer smells. Summer sounds. Why did they make her tremble tonight?

"Help!"

She jumped. The plaintive cry had come from nowhere and yet from everywhere. She whirled wildly, sensing a deadly presence. She sucked in a breath and stared at the dark fringe of trees that circled her home like prison walls.

"Who are you?" she whispered.

A bloodred moon the exact shade of the skull in her nightmare hung over the ranch. Circling it was a bright scarlet ring. She stared at the moon, expecting it to turn into a skull.

She kept watching the moon until it vanished behind a black cloud. She wasn't feeling any easier when a bunch of coyotes began to hoot. Then she heard a man's eerie laughter from beyond the fringe of juniper long after the coyotes stopped.

"Who's out there?" she cried.

The cicadas halted their serenade. A thousand eyes seemed to stare at her from the silent wall of dark trees.

Stark fear drained the blood from her face. She felt like a target.

With a muted cry, she raced back inside her living room with its dozens of velvet floral paintings and cozy, overstuffed furniture.

Slamming her door, she flipped on all her lights. Then she stared unseeingly at the sofa piled high with her recent purchases from a flea market—mirrored sunglasses, towel sets, children's clothes and toys, all in need of sorting. Breathing heavily, she triple-bolted the door and sagged against it.

Maybe the moon hadn't been a human skull floating above the house, but one thing was for sure—she'd never seen anything like that bloodred moon circled with a ring of fire before. Never in all her sixty-six years.

And that cry for help. And the laughter—that terrible, inhuman laughter coming from the trees…

Someone was out there. Someone with murder in his heart.

Rosita could trace her blood to prehistoric civilizations in Mexico. She knew in her bones that this moon was a sign.

The Fortunes were in trouble—again.

She'd worked for them for a long time. Too long, Ruben said. He wanted her to retire so she could focus on him. "We'll move away, not too far, but we'll have a place of our own."

Ruben had always wanted his own land, but she

loved Ryan Fortune and his precious wife, Lily, as if
they were members of her own family. She couldn't
leave them. Not now! Not when she knew they needed
her more than ever. In the morning she would try to warn
them as she cooked them eggs and bacon and tamales
and frijoles. They teased her because she cooked frijoles
with every meal.

They would probably laugh at her for warning them,
too. Ryan and Lily had loved each other since they
were kids, but they'd had to wait a lifetime to realize
their love. They wanted to be happy, and she wanted
that for them, too. Why, then, did her heart feel heavy
with the thought that they were doomed? Oh, dear.
Maybe when the sun was high in the sky tomorrow she
would be able to laugh at her fears and believe all would
be well.

She made a fist. "I have to tell them anyway! First
thing, when I go to the ranch house!"

When she finally stopped shaking, it was a long time
before she felt safe enough to switch off a few of the
lights. Even then she was still too nervous to go back to
bed or to sort through her flea market purchases, so she
curled up in her favorite armchair and clutched the arm-
rests as if her life depended on it.

The night seemed endless. If only she could wake
Ruben and tell him about the skull and the laughter.

But he would only think her stupid. He would tell her
it was nothing and order her to bed. Because he was a
man, he thought he knew everything.

"*Ya verás.* You'll see, *viejo.* You'll see when somebody dies," she whispered, hugging herself as the shad-

owy forms of the tall furniture in her living room shaped themselves into snakes and cougars and alligators.

Somebody was going to die!

Soon.

As soon as they reached the Double Crown Ranch, everything would be under control again, and he could focus on his plan to get even with Ryan Fortune.

The man who was driving fought to stay calm. He was as unnerved by his passenger as he was by the automatic with the silencer he'd concealed under his own floor mat, which felt like a lump under his left heel.

He disliked guns, but he liked order. He had to have everything in its exact place. His slacks were all hung together in his closet; his shoes were in shoe racks. The gun was a tool to help restore order. That was all. That was why he'd had plastic surgery, why he'd come to Texas.

Neither moon nor stars lit the wild, desolate ranch land that was owned by the man he was determined to destroy. Except for the twin cones of light arcing every time he struck a pothole or an overlarge rock and except for the interior lights of the big car, the passenger and driver were lost in a strange, pink-tinted, black void that seemed as deep and dark and endless as outer space.

"What the hell are you doing down here in Texas?" his passenger whispered in a low, raw tone from his side of the car.

The driver was tempted to brag about his clever plan. Instead he bit his lips as he whipped down the gravel county road at an even faster speed, sending rocks flying into the dark encroaching walls of cedar and oak.

One of his large, perfectly manicured, suntanned hands gripped the steering wheel; the other held a silver flask half filled with vodka. Both fists were white knuckled and shaking.

"You shouldn't have run out in the middle of those psychological tests," the passenger said in that cool, kindly voice that sent chills through him.

The hell I need more psychological testing!

"What do you know about it?" the driver muttered, his body rigid. "I'm fine. I'm just fine."

"Then why'd you come here? Why'd you change your face? If I didn't know you, I wouldn't have recognized you." There was anguish and what sounded like genuine concern in his passenger's voice.

Not being recognizable was the point, of course. "Like I told you, I was in an accident."

"Why are you stalking these people?"

The driver forced himself to take a calming breath before he replied. "You think you're so smart! You always act so nice! What do you know about anything? About me?"

"I have to try to help you—for your own good."

The driver's mouth went dry. He could taste his fear.

Yes. His unwanted visitor could ruin everything...if he didn't tidy things up fast.

When they rumbled over a cattle guard, every bump seemed to trigger an electric current that snapped up and down the driver's legs and spine. Thoroughly shaken, he could barely control the big car as it raced almost blindly down the narrow road through buttery-thick pockets of Hill Country ground fog before it burst out of the murk into the warm, black night again.

"Slow down," his passenger ordered. "Are you crazy? You could hit a deer or wrap us around a tree."

The driver lifted his flask and sipped the burning liquor as his silent brain screamed shrilly. Who do you think you are—giving me orders? You? You! Ever since we were kids? And calling me crazy?

"Sure," he replied easily as his toe tapped a little harder on the accelerator. "I'll slow down. Sure I will. Hey, relax. We're nearly there."

"You don't want me here, do you?" came that kindly, superior, all-knowing voice. "I could tell. Your eyes were colder than chips of black marble when you opened your door tonight. But I didn't come to scare you or hurt you."

"Scared? Who's scared? If I seemed upset, maybe you should have called first."

"Right. Give you time to roll out the welcome mat." His passenger laughed.

The driver rubbed his brow where the scars from his accident should have been. Then he took another sip from the flask. Not too much. He didn't want to alarm his passenger by acting any more nervous than he had to. Slowly he dropped his hand back to the seat. He had to focus. He had to concentrate.

"No. You didn't want me here," his passenger insisted, again in that hateful, kindly, yet all-knowing tone that the driver loathed.

The moon broke out of the cloud cover, and instantly the driver wished it hadn't. The bloodred globe was huge and obscene and ringed with flame. Strange-looking, crimson-stained clouds scudded beneath it.

He'd never seen anything like it. Was it even real? Or was it just the mad, blistering fury throbbing in his temples that made it seem so ominous? Was he that charged on adrenaline?

No sooner had it appeared, than the livid moon vanished, leaving the night blacker than pitch again.

His lips felt dry, as did his throat. Every cell in his being screamed with the need to drain the whole damn flask. But he didn't dare take even the shortest pull. He knew he was close to some fatal edge.

Later he could drink all he wanted.

Later. When it was over. When he felt brave and strong—when he was safe again. Later he would gloat about tonight, about how smart he'd been when he'd played this hand. Later he would review his clever revenge plot, too.

Later, after drinks and sex. Lots of sex with a woman who was good at it. Thinking about sex with *her,* thinking about what she would do to him with her hands and lips, cooled his temper just enough.

"Of course I want you here," he lied smoothly, whipping the steering wheel to the right so fast the car skidded and spit gravel. "It's just that I've got a lot on my mind."

"Slow down." The voice in the shadowy car was razor sharp now.

"All right." The driver slammed on the brakes, and the car spun crazily in the gravel, throwing them toward the dash, before it stopped.

"Where the hell are we?" his passenger demanded.

"The Double Crown Ranch."

"I don't believe you. Where's the house?"

"Over there." He pointed. "See the light? Just through the trees."

The juniper and oak were a solid mass of darkness. Still, a faint glow of silver had been visible seconds before.

"What are you trying to pull this time?"

He dug under the floor mat. Grabbing the big automatic, he pointed it at the other man's belly. "Shut up and get out of the car!"

"What?"

"Now!"

"I want to talk to Ryan Fortune."

"All in good time."

"I came here to help you. I told people where I was going and whom I was coming to see."

"Sure you did."

The driver was smiling and yanking out the keys and opening his own door all at the same time. The other man lunged, grabbing the hand that held the gun.

"Bastard!" The driver threw him off and catapulted out of the car onto the sharp, limestone rocks. Vaguely he was aware of cicadas singing in the trees, aware too of the warm, sultry, summer heat.

The other man sprang on top of him and wrapped his wide hands around the wrist that held the gun and squeezed. Still, somehow the driver managed to lift the automatic and smash it onto his assailant's brow.

The other man collapsed, blood pouring down his

face. His body sagged to the ground as limply as a heavy bag of feed.

The driver bent over him. "Always acting nice when all you've ever wanted was to destroy me."

"I...I came here to help you."

Holding the gun close to his assailant's head, the driver smiled. "Thanks." He pulled the trigger. Once. Twice.

And then again, just to make sure. He shot him right between the eyes the last time, eyes that were soft and pleading and almost the same color as his own.

The other man lay where he'd fallen, soundless, still. The driver rolled away from the body to avoid the awful rush of blood that flowed from the back of his head and drenched the hard, dry earth.

Slowly the killer pulled himself to his feet. Funny, how the suffocating night smelled sweet and woodsy again. Funny, how the cicadas never let up. Summer bugs. How he loved summer bugs.

Suddenly he felt light-headed, dizzy. A strange weakness in his muscles made him fall to his knees again. Shock? Revulsion?

In the next moment his stomach heaved, and he threw up all over his expensive shirt and slacks. For a long moment he was too weak to stand.

Visions of the dead man when he'd been a boy bombarded his mind. He remembered the cool, bright day they'd learned to ride bikes together. He never would have gotten the hang of it if the dead man hadn't encouraged him.

Don't think about the past.

His mind raced. He had to get out of here.

But the body…

He couldn't leave the body at the Double Crown Ranch. He had to dump it somewhere.

Where? Where? His mind raced in panic-stricken circles.

He grabbed his flask out of the car and drained the last of the vodka. He threw it down. Then he picked it up and tossed it into the car.

Lake Mondo, he thought dully. Water destroyed evidence. He'd wash himself off there, too, before anybody saw him.

His heart was thundering in his chest and throat as he got up, still weaving drunkenly. When he caught his breath, he grabbed the body by the legs and began tugging it over the rocks toward the trunk of his car.

When a band of coyotes began to yelp, the driver laughed out loud along with them, and once he started hooting, he couldn't stop, even after the coyotes did.

Suddenly he was aware of a listening, knowing presence. He stopped laughing and stared at the dark trees that surrounded him.

If there'd been a light in the trees, it had damn sure gone out now. Whoever or whatever had been there couldn't have seen much.

He threw the body in the trunk, inspected the ground with a flashlight and then drove off in a hurry, little caring that his tires spun gravel. The stench of fresh vomit was so powerful he had to roll all the windows down to keep from gagging.

There was no one to stop him now. Now he could

focus on his clever plan to topple that self-serving, arrogant bastard, Ryan Fortune, who saw himself as the king of Texas.

One

Austin, Texas

Why do people visit graves when there's nobody here?

Amy Burke-Sinclair's long, slim fingers involuntarily knotted around the steering wheel of her Toyota Camry.

Lush green lawns peppered with neat tombstones stretched into the hazy distance as Amy followed the familiar, narrow lane that wound through cedar and oak. At this early hour the sun that could be brutal by midday was no more than a soft orange ball peeping timidly above the horizon, sending long, purple shadows across this perfectly manicured, emerald patch of earth.

Not that its sleeping inhabitants knew or cared.

Not that Lexie cared.

Amy imagined Lexie's gray face inside her casket

and flinched. Again her hands tightened as she fought for some happier image.

She saw Lexie galloping beside her on her colt, Smoky, her red hair flying behind her as she leaned forward. She saw her slow dancing in skintight jeans with a drink in one hand and a cigarette in the other on the deck of her parents' lake house that last night.

Amy swallowed a deep, ragged breath. As always, memories of Lexie alive brought even more guilt than thoughts of her in her grave.

Amy hadn't seen any other cars or even pedestrians in the cemetery. Which was good. She couldn't have endured another accidental meeting with Robert Vale, Lexie's father.

Last year they'd come at the same time. He'd seen her and walked over to her car, stiffly handsome in a pressed black suit. He'd smiled, but his silver eyes hadn't.

"I'm sorry," she'd said, unable to look at him. "So sorry."

"The hell you are. I'll call and tell your mother I saw you here. Then you'll be sorry."

"Please…"

Robert Vale had given her a single, killing glance before he'd stridden over to his own car and started it. He'd called her mother, and her mother had called her.

"Why can't you just do as you're told?" she'd said. "Just stay away from that grave. How difficult is that?"

"I…I didn't even get out of my car."

"That's something I suppose."

Rebellion at her mother's criticism had flared briefly

inside Amy. Then her mother had said, "Dear, you've got to let this go."

Eight years. Today all Amy felt was numbness and coldness. She was like a robot instead of grief-stricken as she should be. Never once since the accident had she shed a single tear.

She didn't think she ever would. It was as if something in her had died that wild night eight years ago. And yet she hadn't died. Lexie had.

She'd been the lucky one.

When Amy reached the gate to Lexie's grave, she braked. Rolling down the windows, she gave a long, hollow sigh. Her heart ached. A minute passed before her shaky fingers managed to touch the icy keys. With an effort she forced herself to cut the engine.

Instantly the air felt dense and close. The car's interior warmed up fast as the awful stillness of the cemetery wrapped around her.

Amy, who was an events planner, had back-to-back meetings all day. The powerful, demanding man whose account she was representing right now had an incredibly active personal life and career. Sometimes she felt as if she was his number-one gopher.

She twisted a strand of her long, blond hair around a fingertip. Being busy and keeping herself surrounded with people were her drugs of choice. Constant work and constant people kept the real demons at bay—at least, most of the time. Her number-one client called her night and day. That was a good thing.

On nights when she hadn't pushed herself to the point of exhaustion, her demons attacked her full force.

Sometimes she saw Lexie's face in a deep pool of water with her red hair flowing all around her. Sometimes she heard Lexie's laughter. Sometimes she dreamed she was riding endlessly over dark water, calling Lexie's name.

As she had so many times in the past, Amy tried to pray. She squeezed her eyes shut, but her heart felt too numb. Instead of forming coherent thoughts, her mind went blank.

"God, please hear my silent cry," she finally whispered in despair as her hopelessness consumed her.

Opening her eyes, Amy caught the funereal scent of roses. She sighed again and let go of her hair. Eight lush, velvety red blossoms wrapped in pink tissue lay on the leather seat beside her cell phone. The flowers had been expensive. She'd meant to give them to Lexie. This time she'd really meant to get out and walk up to her grave.

She still meant to, only when she leaned across the seat and lifted the bouquet, a thorn pricked her through the tissue paper. Then just as she touched the door handle, her cell phone rang. She picked it up.

She tensed when she read *Carole Burke* in vivid blue. Mother.

Amy frowned and set the phone back down. When it finally stopped ringing, she touched the door handle. Again her hand froze, just as it always did, and her throat went tight and scratchy.

Folding her hands in her lap, she just sat there for several more minutes and endured the silence and the heat that intensified the sickly fragrance of the roses, until finally she tossed them onto the backseat. They would wilt and turn black before she noticed them again.

As she started the Camry, she was almost glad about the long, stressful day ahead of her, almost glad she was going out to dinner tonight with Betsy. At least she wouldn't be home alone on this night of all nights, her thirtieth birthday.

Thirty. She was thirty.

Eight years ago Lexie had given her a wild birthday party on Lake Mondo. Amy hadn't had another birthday party since. She never even let her parents bake her a cake.

Even so, she had to go out tonight, not to celebrate, but to avoid her mother's calls, to avoid the empty walls of her apartment and the awful silence, as well. And the dreams. She couldn't face her dreams.

Thirty. She was thirty.

She was alive…and yet in some ways, she felt less alive than Lexie.

Damn! Steve Fortune knew he wasn't much of a cook. Hell, he was supposed to be the *owner* of this establishment, not the cook. Try telling that to Amos, who hadn't shown up on the busiest night of the week.

Steve's left forefinger throbbed where he'd just burned it frying hamburger patties. He needed a beer—fast—to soothe his frayed nerves.

It was ladies' night at the Shiny Pony Bar and Grill on Sixth Street in Austin, Texas, and so, as usual, his trendy bar was jammed with beautiful women seeking cheap booze and the admiration of urban cowboys who showed up to amuse them.

Men like me, he thought cynically. Steve was thirty-six, too old for this sort of mating game. Too smart, too.

After all, he was the smart triplet. At least, that's the story he tried to sell his brothers.

The girls with their long, satiny hair and their slim hips encased in skintight jeans looked young as they stood at the sturdy wooden bar beside all the liquor and fancy glasses that were stacked sky high. Hell, these girls looked way too young and naive for what he had in mind.

Madison.

Why the hell had Madison chosen to show up this morning on Cabot's arm when they met to sign the formal papers? She'd had that wounded look in her eyes that carved out his heart and made Steve wonder if Cabot was taking care of her.

She's not your responsibility anymore.

Sucking on his blistered finger, Steve sank into an out-of-the-way booth where he could watch the action in the shadow-filled room charged with an overload of testosterone and estrogen. The dark lighting, high ceilings, huge beams and scuffed, wood floors made for a cozy, casual atmosphere.

He should have fired Amos for being late again. It was the third time in thirty days. But Steve had been desperate to have a night off, so he'd merely nodded when Amos had finally shown up. He'd ripped off his grease-spattered apron and tossed it at the redheaded kid with too many piercings. Then Amos had mouthed the usual apologies for oversleeping again. Hell, Steve was a softie when it came to firing people.

"Don't make it a habit," Steve had warned, barely

holding on to his temper before he'd slammed out of the swinging doors of his kitchen.

Steve hated calls on his cell at the end of a long day at his ranch to come pinch hit at the Shiny Pony Bar and Grill. He hated being dependent on irresponsible kids like Amos. He wanted out of the restaurant/bar business. The sooner, the better! Not that the Shiny Pony didn't coin money, but it took management. Hell, he wouldn't have a ranch if it weren't for this place. There was big money in a trendy bar, but if Steve wasn't here all the time, his help got creative. Real creative. Either they didn't show or cash, booze and food evaporated into thin air.

A vision of Madison—blond, golden with pain-filled eyes—arose before him. God, she'd looked great this morning in that white silk suit with her golden hair swept sleekly back from her thin face.

Steve signaled Jeff, his number-one bartender, for a beer. After a beer, or maybe two, he wanted a woman, preferably a brainless, buxom brunette with a bad-girl body she knew what to do with. Next he wanted to take all his phones off the hook, read his book about ancient Greek wars and get a good night's sleep, preferably alone, so he'd be fresh for his meeting with the governor tomorrow morning. If that was ruthless, he had his reasons—*reason*.

Madison.

Not that Steve was in a rush to pick up a bimbo. Truth to tell, such women bored the hell out of him. After all, he was supposed to be the intellectual in his family. The smart triplet. He dreaded the preliminary flirtations and idiotic maneuvers necessary to bed such a woman.

Hey, smart triplet, idiocy and boredom equal self-preservation.

Still wearing his jeans, work boots and sweat-stained Stetson, he leaned back in the tall, dark booth while he grimly eyed the pretty women clustered around little tables and booths. When a beautiful young brunette at the bar, who was braless in a tank top, smiled at him, he frowned until he saw Jeff flying toward his table with a frosty mug of Corona.

"Here you go, boss. Three slices of lime just the way you like it."

"Thanks."

Steve squeezed the limes and then took a slow swig of beer. The familiar knots in his muscles meant he was exhausted from a long day at his ranch, followed by his stint of playing stand-in cook after Jeff had called him. After signing papers at his lawyer's office, where he'd seen Madison, Steve had spent the morning arguing with construction crews about the delays in the restoration of his historical ranch house. At noon his meeting with his architect and contractor had been tense, to say the least.

In less than six months he would be hosting the big, prestigious, annual Hensley-Robinson Awards Banquet because this year the governor had chosen to honor Ryan Fortune, who just happened to be Steve's good friend, distant cousin and mentor.

His damn house *had* to be ready. What could he do to make James, his laid-back, good-ol'-boy contractor, who liked to hunt and fish at least once a week and every sunny weekend, understand that?

Then there was Dixon. Dixon was turning into a helluva pest. Steve had wasted the afternoon in the hot sun watching men survey the pastures of his legendary ranch, the Loma Vista, because Dixon, his neighbor to the east, was disputing the one-hundred-year-old fence line between the properties.

Dixon had wanted to buy the ranch himself. He'd given Steve trouble about the title ever since Steve had bought the place from old Mel Foster.

Not that Steve wanted to rehash his day. Hell, he wanted to forget it. He'd intended to celebrate an anniversary of sorts and a victory and then to party with the lady of his choice.

The Shiny Pony Bar and Grill was now his, all his. As of this morning, no more meetings with Larry Cabot, his former partner and former best friend. Betraying best friend, he reminded himself. No more Madison Beck, either. He was done once and for all with her, even if she was his ex-fiancée, whom he'd loved. Hell, she'd broken his heart exactly one year ago to the day.

Would he ever forget standing at the altar, waiting for her, all eyes drilling him while "Here Comes the Bride" was played for the fifth time?

Steve forced a deep breath. Finally he could close the book on the sorry chapter of his life in which Cabot and Madison had starred.

Steve had told everybody who would listen that he resented her for jilting him for Cabot, his former college buddy, who'd been born with more money than God, as had four generations of Cabots before him.

So why did he ache every time he even thought about Madison? Because she was lovely and so vulnerable, he still worried about her. Because she needed to be told and shown constantly that she was beautiful and loved. Cabot was too arrogant to tend to anyone's needs other than his own.

Steve had wanted to take care of her for the rest of their lives. Her parents had died when she was eight, leaving her to grow up poor and abandoned. Underneath her glamorous facade, she'd been a scared little girl in need of love. He'd been determined to make her feel safe. As it had turned out, money represented real security to her.

Cabot and he had owned a couple of restaurants with bars downtown. Steve had bought out Cabot's interest in this place while selling him his own interest in the Lonesome Saloon, which, unfortunately, was just across the street. From time to time, he would probably run into Cabot. Only, now they wouldn't have to speak or work together. He probably wouldn't see much of Madison anymore.

Even as his heart ached, Steve's mouth twisted. "Cheers," he growled in a low voice as his callused hand tightened on the handle of his mug.

"Goodbye, Madison." With a supreme effort he lifted his mug and willed her to stop haunting him.

One day at a time. One night at a time. That had been his mantra ever since his screwed-up wedding day. His triplet brothers, Miles and Clyde, who ribbed him about everything, still hadn't dared to even breathe Madison's name in his presence or mention the wedding. Jack, his older brother, whom Steve had idolized as a child, had suffered too much heartbreak himself to ever embarrass Steve about his.

Steve glanced toward the long-haired brunette at the bar in the tight red tank top. The skinny blond kid who was standing beside her kept edging his drink closer to hers. If Steve wanted her, he'd better get a move on.

To hell with her.

"No woman will ever turn me into a chump like that again," he vowed aloud, addressing the brunette, who smiled at him and batted her lashes even as she leaned against the kid, nudging his bulging bicep with her breast.

To hell with her. The last thing Steve would ever do was pick a fight with a paying customer over a woman.

Steve glanced away—straight into the haunted eyes of a smoldering golden-haired, golden-skinned babe, who at first glance seemed an exact replica of Madison.

Run!

She stared straight into his eyes and held them and him perfectly still for an endless moment.

His pulse quickened.

No blondes, you fool.

He told himself that smart guys learned from their mistakes.

Smart or not, his blood coursed through him like a molten rush. Blondes, not to mention Madison clones, were no-no's, and the little voices in his head began shouting all the familiar warnings.

The blonde crossed her long legs and then uncrossed them, very very slowly. Her black spandex skirt was so short, he got a glimpse of matching black lace panties.

Mesmerized, Steve let his gaze crawl up her legs. When she oozed forward on her bar stool, her glossy red smile widened. He could not stop staring at her—at her lips, at her body. He kept hoping against hope she'd shift her position on that damn stool and uncross and cross those gorgeous legs again. He wanted more of those thighs and black lace.

Her companion was a stunning black girl with big hair and skin the color of caramel. A tight red sheath hugged her slim body. Gold bangles gleamed at her throat and ears. When she caught him watching the blonde, she winked sassily and shot him a toothy grin. Then a cowboy came up to her and asked her to dance. She melted into the tall man's arms, leaving the coast clear for Steve. When she began to undulate on the dance floor, everybody in the bar except Steve watched her.

Through narrowed dark eyes, Steve refocused on the blonde. She was slender, rather than voluptuous, classy looking in spite of her skimpy outfit.

In the right clothes, say a white silk suit like the one Madison had worn this morning, she would fit on his arm anywhere. He could even take her home to meet Mom in Manhattan and the brothers.

Squash that thought.

Her creamy, honey-colored skin—thanks to low-cut black spandex, he could see a lot of that, too—and her rippling yellow hair looked so soft he wanted to wrap her body around his and carry her out to the back alley and take her against a wall caveman style. He wanted to smother his face in her hair and then rip that little nothing of a skirt off and yank down her panties. He wanted to touch her, to kiss her, to taste her—now. He wanted her mouth on his body, kissing him everywhere. He wanted her so badly, he knew he should run.

Why *her?* Her narrow face wasn't conventionally pretty. Her mouth was too large, her slender nose too long, her cheekbones too high and pronounced. She was too tall probably and too slim for him, as well. But her big sad eyes that tilted upward at the corners lured him in some unfathomable way.

The voices in his head had given up. As he shoved his Stetson back, Steve's gaze drifted from the blonde's mouth to her small, firm breasts, down her waist, down her hips and then lower, skimming the length of her long, tanned legs again. She wore black cowboy boots embroidered with red roses. He knew boots. Hers were custom-made.

She broke the gaze, releasing him. Then she puckered her wet, shiny mouth and slowly bent forward so that her breasts, small as they were, bulged enticingly as she blew out the birthday candle on the tiny chocolate cupcake he hadn't noticed before in the middle of the little round table.

Hell, was that a tiny tattoo above her left breast?

It sure as hell was. He hated tattoos. So would Mom. So would his triplet brothers.

Forget Mom and Clyde and Miles.

Her black-lashed eyes lifted to his again, and her mouth curved when she realized he was still watching her.

She was something all right. And she knew it. She was good at this. She probably trolled somewhere different every night.

The cowboy to his right was giving her the eye, too. Jealousy washed Steve in a hot green wave. In that black spandex miniskirt and the low-cut black blouse with hunky coral jewelry at her throat and wrists, she was the hottest woman in the bar. If he didn't go after her, some other guy sure as hell would.

Steve's hand on his mug froze. Her enormous light-colored eyes were too sweet and sad for words.

She looked lost—just like Madison had this morning. Just like his brother Jack used to after Ann's death. Suddenly Steve wanted very badly to know why she was hurting. Even though he didn't want to be involved, he felt connected, which meant he should run. He removed his Stetson, placed it on the table and ran his hands through his short dark-brown hair. Then he took a long pull from his mug.

He wanted her. Only her. Maybe because he couldn't have Madison. The situation scared the hell out of him. Still, he said the predictable sort of prayer all horny bastards say in bars after a beer or two when they see a pretty woman they want.

Please, make her a nymphomaniac. At least for tonight.

He hoped the Man Upstairs was listening. Tightening his grip on his beer, he shoved back from his table and arose awkwardly.

Time to make his move.

As he swaggered toward her, his boots thudding heavily on the rough wooden boards, he felt like an actor in a bad play. Ever since his fatal wedding day, crowds gave him claustrophobia. The closer he got to her, the more the other people in the bar seemed to stare.

He wasn't even halfway across the room when the walls started pressing closer and his breathing grew labored. He was gulping for air when another cowboy on the way to the bar shoved him, jarring him back to reality.

The voices in his head began to scream. *No blondes, dummy. No blondes.*

"Sorry," the cowboy said with a sheepish grin.

"Sure," Steve grunted as his throat squeezed shut.

Jeff signaled him.

No way could he talk to the blonde now.

Beyond Jeff, he saw an exit sign. Blindly he veered toward it, stumbled over a chair leg and sent two chairs flying. When he righted them, his legs felt heavier. Every step was impossibly difficult. He felt as if he was slogging through knee-deep mud.

Hell.

"Wait! Your hat!" a velvet voice cried behind him.

He turned and saw the black girl in the red sheath waving his Stetson at him.

To hell with his hat! He'd buy another one.

Then the blonde snatched it out of her friend's hand and slowly put it on. It was way too big for her, but she looked cuter than hell when she peeped at him from underneath the brim with her huge, lost eyes.

Her mouth curved in a sweet, sad smile that made

Two

Amy felt flushed. Was it the Flirtita, a fruity variation of a Margarita, that she was drinking that was making her feel light-headed and bolder than usual? Or was it the wild drumbeat of the music pulsing inside her like a second heartbeat?

"Wait!" Rasa yelled.

Amy couldn't believe Rasa. She was too much. When the tall, dark cowboy didn't answer the impossible girl or turn around, Rasa strolled back to Amy's table with his hat, her pretty mouth petulant.

"He's leaving! I can't believe your hot-to-trot cowboy is galloping for the hills! You'd better get up and take him his hat, baby."

Amy jumped up and then forced herself to sit back down.

She *wanted* to run after him.

The evening was definitely out of control, and that scared Amy, who was into control—normally.

"I don't know what got into me. Coming here…with you…tonight of all nights. And flirting with him. What am I doing here?"

Amy slapped her own cheek so hard it stung. She had to get a grip, if not on Rasa, on herself.

"It's your birthday. You're thirty. You're having a Margarita."

"A Flirtita," Amy corrected. "Specialty of the house. And it's strong. Too strong."

Or maybe it just seemed strong because she hadn't had any alcohol for eight years.

"Maybe I'll try one." When Rasa held up her hand to signal a waiter, Amy grabbed her wrist and lowered it.

"Oh, no, you don't."

"So, what's wrong with flirting a little when a guy's *that* cute?"

I could tell you what's wrong. If you had my memories, you'd understand.

"You might as well be dead if you don't live a little," Rasa said, waving his hat at him again.

Dead.

The charged word echoed in Amy's bruised heart and soul as she shakily sipped her Flirtita and tried to pretend all she felt was a haughty nonchalance. She wasn't about to tell Rasa, whom she barely knew, about her visit to the cemetery, which was partly why she felt so crazy and out of control tonight.

When Rasa waved the cowboy hat again, Amy

jumped up and grabbed it. "Would you stop?" The room whirled. She *had* to quit sipping this delicious drink.

The hat was still warm and damp around the head-band because he'd worn it and worked in it. She caught the sharp, masculine scent of his cologne. Hardly know-ing what she did, Amy flipped the battered hat over and then glanced toward him again. Without even realizing her intention, she put it on her head. When it sank to midbrow, she spun it around on her head, feeling like a kid playing dress-up.

Oh, God, what was she doing? Making a pass at a... stranger? Wearing his hat? She should have known the last place she should have come to was a cowboy bar with posters of cowgirls riding horses on the walls, not to mention Flirtitas. The posters and the sweet fruit drink mixed with vodka had made her feel crazy. All of a sud-den she was remembering how it felt to be young and to ride like the wind under a blazing sun. To be happy. To trust in the beauty of life itself. To feel immortal.

Amy's hand tightened around the stem of her cold, wet glass. She had no right to flirt with anybody ever, even if he was dark and broad-shouldered and the hunk-iest guy she'd seen in years.

Flirtita or no Flirtita, hunk or no hunk, she couldn't lose control. She was damaged and dangerous and therefore determined never to hurt anybody else, not even herself, ever again.

"Look," she began softly, removing his hat and plac-ing it very firmly on the table. "Rasa, I don't come to bars. I don't pick up strange men. Especially not cow-boys. I work. That's all I do."

"Why not cowboys? You prejudiced or something?"

"No. It's because—" She looked up into Rasa's dark, imploring eyes. "Just because."

"Okay, so you met one bad cowboy."

"No!" You don't understand. Again, she felt too near some dangerous edge. Defiantly Amy swirled her Flirtita glass so vigorously the liquid flashed like angry fire.

"Are you going to punish yourself forever?"

"You don't understand."

"Betsy has told me a little."

"Really? Well, she doesn't know the half of it, okay?"

"Not okay. Baby, he's still watching you while he talks to that bartender. It's not too late. Maybe you should go over there and—"

"No."

"You should definitely lighten up."

"If I do that, anything could happen."

"So let it."

Amy set her glass down by the beige Stetson. He'd looked so handsome in that rumpled hat. So dark and virile and absolutely adorable. Intending to push the hat away, she pulled it toward her and stroked the brim with a trembling fingertip.

"You're way too serious," Rasa persisted.

Why should I listen to advice from someone I've known all of two hours? Someone who doesn't have a clue what kind of person I really am?

"You should try to be friendly." Rasa's hand squeezed hers gently. "Maybe then you'd meet some interesting people and move on." Her voice softened. "Betsy says you bury yourself alive."

"Maybe I don't want to move on."

"Or maybe you just need a helping hand."

Amy yanked her hand free and drained the last of her Flirtita. "Betsy's a big one to talk."

"Hey, he just looked at you again."

Amy didn't smile or look his way or even look at Rasa, who was staring at her way too intently now. The words *dead* and *bury* had Amy too tense and scared to think what she should do. She had to get out of here. She had to get back to her safe, controlled life.

"Rasa, you said one drink and we'd go to dinner."

"And I haven't finished my drink."

"Because you won't drink it."

Rasa laughed.

"If only Betsy were here," Amy said.

"You wouldn't be here if Betsy were here. You two would be at that boring restaurant she told me about. You'd be taking a rash of heat over the cell phone from your number-one client, and she'd be reading her book."

"Exactly."

"Ouch." Rasa laughed.

Betsy Pinkley, Amy's best friend, who had mousy brown hair and thick glasses and who was even duller than she was, if that were possible, had ditched her to stay home and read because her allergies had flared up.

Tonight when Amy had dropped by Betsy's apartment to pick her up, a red-eyed Betsy had been sitting on her couch in her pajamas dabbing tissues at her running eyes and nose.

"It's the cedar again. I'm too sick to go out," she'd

said miserably. "But not to worry. I didn't call you because Rasa can go with you instead."

"Rasa? I don't know a Rasa."

"My next-door neighbor's baby sister." Betsy had
blown her nose messily and then plucked handfuls of
tissues from the box beside. "Rasa's from out of town.
Her brother Trell had a date, and she's dying to see the
action on Sixth Street. So I thought since you want to
go out and she wants to go out…bingo!"

"I don't want to go out with just anybody! And not
to Sixth Street! I want to have dinner with you. Just
you." Amy's cell phone rang. When she saw it was her
mother, she didn't answer it.

"Don't you care that I'm sick at all? I made these special arrangements for you even when my head was killing me."

"Of course I care. But can't you pop an allergy pill?"

"Wait until you meet Rasa," Betsy said.

"I'm leaving." But just as Amy switched off her
cell phone and headed for the door, the bell rang and
Rasa burst inside, only to stop and stare at Amy. Rasa
wore a revealing, low, tight red sheath and lots of gold
bangles while Amy was swathed from head to toe in
gray silk.

"Rasa, this is Amy. Amy—"

"Glad to meet you, baby, but, hey… I thought we
were gonna have some fun tonight. What's with the
gray shroud?" She turned to Betsy. "How come you
didn't tell me your friend was a nun?"

"What?" Amy said. "Now I'm being stood up and
insulted!"

Rasa rolled her almond-shaped eyes. "Hey, sorry. Sometimes I come on a little strong."

"A little?"

"Sorry. I didn't mean to hurt your feelings. You're great looking. The question is—why are you hiding that fact?" Rasa lifted her brows and then walked around Amy, studying her figure closely. "Lucky for you, we're about the same size. I bought a couple of hot new outfits this afternoon that will do wonders for you."

"I…I don't do hot." Amy felt the blood drain from her face as guilt squeezed her chest in a vise. It had been a long time since she'd worn dramatic clothes to draw attention to herself. Lately, though, she'd been sick of her dull wardrobe. "Truly, all I want is a quiet dinner."

Instead of listening, Rasa raced outside. Amy heard a car door slam. Then Rasa burst inside again. She was as quick in her movements and thought processes as Lexie had been.

Amy couldn't help being reminded of Lexie's laughing face as she'd jumped into the boat that last, fatal night.

Rasa ripped open a paper bag and held up two spandex skirts and blouses the size of postage stamps. "Aren't they just darling?"

Lexie would have loved them. The old Amy would have loved them.

"Black spandex?" Amy said.

"This new look will do wonders for you."

"I am not wearing that."

"Thanks, darlin', for guarding my hat in this den of iniquity."

The deep, male drawl cut into Amy's thoughts, and

she jumped, sloshing her Flirtita all over her right hand and his hat.

His quick grin was wolflike. She felt her face flame with unwanted pleasure even before his large hand lifted the damp Stetson from her table and placed it on his head. "Fits me better than it does you," he drawled softly as he picked up a napkin and handed it to her. "Looks better on you, though, darlin'."

Hot and cold chills raced through her body as she dabbed at her hand.

He leaned over her shoulder. "Would you like to dance?" he whispered into her ear. His warm breath stirring the golden tendrils against her earlobe sent wild, tingly sensations down her spine as glass and cutlery tinkled somewhere nearby. The heat of her body stirred her, too.

"N-no!"

"All right, then. Just thought I'd ask." He grinned his big-bad-wolf grin. "See ya 'round."

He turned, and she found herself gaping with dismay at the breadth of his magnificent, broad shoulders. He was gorgeous. He would ask somebody else. She knew that.

An inexplicable pain knifed her heart. She wouldn't see him ever again. She'd go back to her safe, controlled, workaholic life.

Amy swallowed the lump in her throat. She had to let him go.

"Would you like to sit down?" Rasa quickly invited, causing Amy's heart to leap. "My friend here was just saying she could use another Flirtita."

"I was not!"

"Maybe if she has one, she'll lighten up and dance with me," he said.

Amy couldn't quite suppress her smile.

"She had a tough day," Rasa said. "Real tough. Her boss is rich and famous and demanding. Not to mention she just turned thirty. She could use some sympathy."

The cowboy was staring at Amy again. "Thirty? You don't look twenty."

"I feel thirty."

"Bye, you two," Rasa said, pulling out a chair for him as she winked at Amy. "Have fun! I think I'll go ask somebody cute to dance while you two get to know each other."

Burning color washed Amy's cheeks. "Rasa!"

"It's okay," he said. "I understand. I'll go if you want me to."

His eyes lingered on her face. They reminded her of warm, rich, dark chocolate, at least in color. At the same time, they were hard and shrewd, wary, too.

He seemed vulnerable and almost shy. Was he from the country, in town for a night of fun? If so, what would be the harm of sharing a drink if it went no further than a little flirting?

"No." Was that squeaky, very unsexy sound her voice? "Don't go," she pleaded.

He turned. "You sure?"

No, I'm not sure. I'm the farthest thing from sure. But she said nothing more, and he sat down and signaled a waiter, who came flying to their table to wait on him. Quickly he ordered another round of drinks. Then he turned his full attention back to her.

Close up he was remarkably good-looking, too good-looking, really. Gorgeous even, if one could call such a big, dark, rough-looking man, gorgeous. His body was tall and lean and hard, and he had those wonderfully wide shoulders. His face, with its masculine, angular planes and chiseled cheekbones, was strong. He had thick, dark brows, a long, straight nose, and a full, sensual mouth. He wore a snowy white western shirt with pearl snap buttons.

"Where do you live?" she said, swallowing to wet the dryness in her throat.

"I have a ranch southwest of here."

"I wondered if you were a real cowboy."

"So, the country in me shows."

"Only a little." She laughed, and so did he. She'd once had a thing for cowboys.

"I've been ranching for ten years—among other things. Too many other things. I'd like to start concentrating on the ranching, but I needed to raise capital from my other ventures to buy land and stock."

When she finished her Flirtita, he held up his hand, and the bartender brought her another.

"I really shouldn't."

"It's a hot night," he said. "You feel like dancing with me yet?"

When she gazed at him, his dark face blurred, which meant she'd better dance to burn off that last Flirtita. "Why not?"

He took her hand and led her onto the dance floor. Slowly he folded her into his arms. Then he simply held her against his body for a long time, hesitating, before starting to dance. Still, all too soon they were swaying together to a slow western tune.

She didn't consider herself a good dancer, and she hadn't danced in years. He was sure and masterful even though he danced away from the other couples, who glided past them in a circle. As he held her against his powerful chest and they moved together, she forgot her fear of him and her guilt, at least for the moment. Dancing in his arms was like a drug. Soon her spirits rocketed sky-high.

Although they didn't speak in words, their bodies spoke, and she began to feel more and more at ease with him. Or maybe it was the two Flirtitas. Soon it was as if she'd known him always. Gradually she relaxed, and their bodies became more intimately entwined.

When that song ended, he held her, his heat seeping into her, until the next one, which was a polka, started. Thank God. This time they skipped along expertly with the other dancers until her heart was beating in her throat and her breath began coming faster and faster. He never removed his gaze from her face, nor could she quit looking at him.

They danced to song after song, to waltzes, polkas and two-steps, and each number was more fun than the one before. She felt almost lighthearted. She floated in his arms. When at last the music slowed again, he held her more tightly than before, so tightly that their bodies melted into each other and she felt the hard imprint of his muscular frame molding her softer flesh. He was hot, and his white shirt felt damp. She caught the scent of his spicy aftershave spiked by his own clean scent, which was both musky and pleasantly distinctive.

His holding her with their faces mere inches apart slowly became too erotic to bear.

"You're a good dancer. You must practice. Do you come here often?" she asked, hoping he'd say no.

But he didn't. He crushed her tighter. "I came here to meet somebody just for tonight. But this is different. Don't you know that?" He stroked her throat with a callused thumb, causing a thousand little nerves to tingle delicately.

She gasped.

"You're different," he said. "I think you know that I could care about you...too much."

Hearing the change in his rough voice, Amy glanced up at him. His intense, dark eyes were grave.

"Then you do...come here...often?"

His face was suddenly so serious, her heart ached.

"And do you dance with a different woman every night?"

"If you want to know do I sleep with a lot of different women, just ask me."

"Well, do you?"

"I said you were different." His voice had darkened. "I said I could care. I shouldn't have said that, but I meant it."

"You told me to ask, but you didn't answer. Do you sleep around or not? Am I just tonight's flavor?"

His mouth thinned. He spun her in an intricate turn and then snapped her back into his arms. "If I have in the past, I had my reasons," he growled.

"A man either has character when it comes to women or he doesn't," she said.

"So, things are black-and-white with you, no shades of gray? Good or bad? Evil or virtuous?"

His words sliced her like a knife through soft tissue. She notched her chin up so high, she felt her neck muscles tighten.

"Which are you, then?" he asked. "A saint or a sinner?"

His question stung her like a whip. "You're evading *my* question," she persisted, her tone sharp. "Why is that, I wonder?"

"Maybe because I want you to think well of me." He dragged her closer and bent his dark head down to hers. "What the hell are you running from?"

"You at the moment."

"I don't think so."

When his mouth was less than an inch from hers, she touched his lips with a fingertip.

He sucked the tip into his mouth and suckled it, sending hot, thrilling shivers through her. "You don't have to run from me. I won't hurt you." His voice was husky and his eyes unfocused as he pulled her against him. "I—"

"Wait. Not so fast," she whispered huskily. "I want to know more about you first."

"Okay. So, maybe I've had a few women. They were casual affairs."

"One-night stands?"

"Uncomplicated fun."

"I learned there's no such thing." The weight of her guilt crushed her heart. Why had she said that? Told him anything?

"Really? Then why are you here?"

"I don't know what you mean."

When he lifted her hair back from her hot face, she tried to stop him. She was a little sensitive about her ears, thinking they stuck out too much. Then his mouth brushed her earlobe, and she felt another unwanted rush of heat fire the length of her spine.

"Are you so different from me? Isn't *this* what you came here for?" He kissed her other earlobe.

"This?" she whispered.

"Sex?" he said.

"I for one don't sleep around," she said primly, pulling her hair back over her ears. "I don't go to bars to pick up—"

"You're here. What did you come here for, if not for this?" His lips nibbled her cheek. "You were giving me a look."

The warmth he aroused was so delicious, she gasped. "Don't. I feel faint."

"Has it been that long?"

"Yes."

"Or is it just me?"

"Maybe a little of both," she admitted shyly.

He laughed.

"Don't get conceited."

He kissed her throat above the chunky coral necklace, and she shivered when more heated sensations flared in her stomach. Then she hugged herself with her arms.

"You smell good," he said. "Like flowers."

"Violets," she replied. "Soap and perfume. It was a Christmas gift."

"From a man?"

"From my mother."

He kissed her again, harder than before, and she felt herself responding. Why shouldn't she let him kiss her? Was it so wrong? He'd asked her if she was a saint or a sinner. She was definitely the latter. What would he say if she told him that because of her, her best friend had died and that now she lay in a cold, dark grave Amy couldn't bear to look at?

His mouth made her feel like she was burning up. It wasn't as if she was a virgin, either—although she was, if not technically, a kind of virgin. What was the modern term for it? A born-again virgin. It had been years since that wild time in her life that had ended in disaster. Years. And yet, in a way, that awful time felt like yesterday.

Because she didn't want to think about the cemetery or the past, because she wanted to use him to blot it all out, she arched her left eyebrow flirtatiously. "So, what's your name, cowboy?"

"Steve." With blunt, expert fingers, he cupped her triangular chin. His warm breath fanned tendrils of her hair against her ear.

She relaxed a little as the western music, which was a mournful lament about lost love and death, ebbed and flowed around them.

"Steve," she murmured huskily. "Steve. I've never known a Steve."

"What's yours?"

"Sally, er, Jones."

"Sally?" He bent to kiss her again, and this time she parted her lips. For a long moment his mouth clung to hers. When he fused his body to hers, her heart clamored for even more.

"Take it home, you two. If it's that good, save it for the bedroom," a cowboy quipped as he and his partner glided past them on the dance floor.

"You want to?" Steve asked her. "I've got a hotel room."

"Uncomplicated sex?"

"Maybe, but I wouldn't have called it that."

There's no such thing as uncomplicated sex when two people feel as passionately about each other as we do. Somebody always has an agenda.

"Kiss me first," she murmured, "and I'll decide."

"So this is a test?"

"Of sorts. Scared you won't pass?" She stared teasingly into his dark eyes. "You are scared, aren't you? In spite of all your practice with other women?"

"There haven't been all that many, really," he muttered, looking slightly offended.

He was a lot more arrogant when he was scared, she thought as he nuzzled the side of her throat with his mouth.

"A test, huh? All or nothing? I like that. So you're a risk taker."

"Not a good trait really." She smiled nervously. "And you could decide you don't want me."

"Not a chance, darlin'." His grip tightened on her. "Not a chance in hell."

Thrilled beyond measure at the passion in his determined voice, she felt her heart skip lightly and then pound violently even before his mouth, which was gentle and sweet, claimed hers again. His warm lips slanted across hers, lingering softly until she moaned for more, until she clutched his neck, growing feverish with impatience for him to deepen the kiss.

But he didn't.

"Yes or no?" he whispered on a muted groan, pulling away, nibbling her upper lip before releasing it. "Pass or fail?"

The withdrawal of his mouth touched off a wellspring of hunger in her. Not that she was about to let on.

"You call that a kiss?" she teased, puckering her lips in wanton invitation.

He laughed. "I call it a start of something we can finish later. I like how disappointed you look and sound 'cause I stopped so fast, darlin'. You want more and we both know it."

"Don't flatter yourself."

He let her go. "Well?" His low voice was gruffer. "Yes or no? Pass or fail?"

She pressed her lips tightly against her teeth. "If I say no, will you just start flirting with some other woman?"

He took her hand and brought it to his lips, turning her palm so that he could press his mouth against her flesh. When he did, his kiss sent flames through her.

"Yes or no?" he growled.

Three

"Pass or fail, huh?" she whispered, toying with him as guitars whined and other couples glided past them. "What if I'm still not sure?"

His face was flushed as he clasped her slender waist tighter. His gaze was as intent as a hungry tiger's. "Make up your mind, darlin'. Or do you have another test in mind? You want me to pull some other stunt like stripping or something?"

"No!"

His hands moved to a pearl snap on his white shirt. Swaying to the music, he undid it slowly, and she found herself staring at a virile strip of skin. He looked as wild as a pagan warrior. "Want to see more, darlin'?" He lowered his large hands to the next pearl stud.

"Stop." She covered his hands with her own, inadvertently touching his warm chest. Her fingertips heated instantly, desire flashing through her like quicksilver. Gasping, she would have jumped away if he hadn't grabbed her and held her close.

"Don't break both our hearts by saying no," he murmured.

"Don't be ridiculous. Your heart wouldn't break."

"Darlin', you misjudge me."

The bar was filling up fast. Voices and laughter buzzed around them. A dozen couples joined them on the dance floor. She thought of her empty apartment, of going home alone, of her memories attacking her, when she could have this gorgeous man all to herself.

It had been eight years since the accident. Eight long years since she'd slept with anyone. Not that she'd ever even considered bedding any man this fast. She barely knew Steve, and yet she wanted him so badly she hurt.

This couldn't just be sex, but if it wasn't, somebody would get hurt. Probably him, because she was damaged.

Lexie was dead, and it was her fault.

If I could cause something that terrible, I don't deserve him or even a shred of happiness ever again. Guilt crept over her. How could she forget, even for one night, what her careless, wild behavior had cost?

"What are you so afraid of?" he muttered, ripping at the studs so that his shirt came apart and he stood before her with his hard tanned torso partially exposed. "Touch me. Put your hands on me. I need to feel them on my naked skin."

When still she hesitated, he grabbed her hands and placed them on his chest, on the coarse black hair. Then he began moving them across his hard body until she broke free and clasped him to her around the waist.

He felt as hot as fire, as unyielding as granite.

"I…I don't think we should," she whispered softly, barely able to breathe.

"You think too much."

His voice was anguished rather than angry. She felt his pain. Touching him made her want more, too. Hardly knowing what she was doing, she stood on her tiptoes and moved her arms upward until they circled his neck. With lightning quickness she pulled his face down to hers eagerly and kissed him on the mouth lingeringly. In the next instant he hauled her higher against him, crushing her breasts into his naked chest and her hips against his fully aroused male hardness. If her heart beat wildly against his chest, she felt his pulse thudding even faster than hers.

Somewhere in the depths of her mind, she was aware of his muscles straining on her arms and waist. Then she realized he was half dragging, half carrying her on her tiptoes across the dance floor to the darkest corner in the bar. Once there he pushed her against a wall as if she were no more than a doll and pressed his body into hers.

Again she knew the sweet, dark heat of his mouth as he pleasured her with more kisses, each one more passionate than the last. He was soon rasping deeply between every breath like a hard-run athlete. Nobody had ever kissed her half as greedily. Powerless, she kissed him back, caught in the storm of her own needs. She felt unleashed after years and years of restraint.

Was it him? Was he special? All she knew was that

she wanted him. She wanted him so much she couldn't bear the thought of not having him.

One night. Only one night. A birthday present to myself. Then never again.

With a little moan she parted her lips, and his tongue slid inside. Soon his swollen manhood was a growing pressure against her abdomen. He was huge and tall, and when he held her ever more tightly, she felt her body quiver.

"I want you. I want you more than I ever believed it was possible to want a man."

And you don't even know my real name.

His hands moved over her breasts, and she let him touch her wherever he wanted, her breasts, her buttocks, until she lost all sense of place and time.

"I want you," she repeated.

"You're so beautiful, darlin'. So damned beautiful." He rocked his hips into hers. Arching into him, she felt dizzy and on fire, drunk with the need for more of him.

Suddenly, as abruptly as he'd enticed her, he withdrew, pushing her away, spinning on the tall heels of his black boots and stomping five feet away from her. Quickly he buttoned his shirt and stuffed his shirttail into his jeans. He combed back his hair with quick, rough fingers.

"What are you doing?" she whispered, aching for more kisses as she watched his shaking hand sweep rapidly through his dark hair.

"Pass or fail?" he muttered savagely.

"What?"

"We can't do this here in front of—"

"You're right, of course," she agreed, shamed to the core.

"I own this place," he said.

"You do?"

"All those guys in the white aprons drilling holes in our backs work for me."

"What?"

"I'm done putting on a show for my employees. Besides, if I kiss you, or even so much as touch you again, I don't know what I might be capable of." His dark eyes flashed.

"Then we'd better go," she said, giggling with delight and excitement.

"Pass or fail?" he muttered brusquely.

"How can you ask a dumb question like that when my heart's racing?"

"That's a yes, I take it."

She laughed. "If you don't know that by now, you're not too smart, cowboy. I can barely breathe much less stand."

She slid up beside him, stood on her tiptoes and grabbed his hat, which she put on her own head. Holding the brim, she raced for the exit sign, laughing at him still.

Rasa yelled, "Way to go, Amy." But all Amy focused on was Steve's heavy strides quickening behind her.

She was making a spectacle of herself and of him, and she didn't care. For the first time in years she felt almost her old, young, carefree self—wild and alive and real, free and young and happy.

She didn't deserve real happiness. She knew that. Just as she knew it wouldn't last.

In the morning, this would all be a dream…like it never happened, she promised herself, the demons and Lexie.

She was damaged. The only way to protect her birthday lover would be to leave him.

Outside, hidden in the dark shadows caused by the lush plantings and the wide overhang of the roofline of the Shiny Pony, which was an old Victorian building doing time as a trendy bar, she watched three drunk men shouting at each other in the early-summer heat. She waited until Steve dashed outside and caught up with her.

Sixth Street was iffy at this hour. A woman alone might be okay wandering the streets back to her car. But then again, she might run into an unwanted admirer or several unwanted admirers. Years ago when she and Lexie had sneaked out together to roam the street, they'd been separated. Amy had found herself in a dark alley and had nearly been raped by two young drunks. But Lexie had found them and pounded Amy's attackers in the head with her bag. When that hadn't worked, she'd sprayed them with pepper spray, causing them to run.

The memory made Amy wary. A woman had to be careful. She took off his Stetson and handed it to him. Watching her thoughtfully, he took it and placed it on his head.

"Why the frown?" He touched her elbow, and she jumped back.

"What if I'm not ready to go to your hotel room yet? What if I want to talk?"

He sucked in a breath. "Okay. Where?"

With his brilliantly lit eyes on her, she felt self-conscious all over again. "Over there maybe. The Lonesome Saloon."

Now it was his turn to look wary. His handsome face darkened. "I have a better idea," he said rather edgily. "I'll walk you to your car, and I'll follow you in my truck to the Hyatt. We can have a drink at their bar or walk on the jogging path by Town Lake. Your choice."

"Are you okay?"

Instead of answering her, he took a long breath, shot her a reassuring smile that didn't fool her and said, "Where the hell's your car?"

It was obvious he didn't want to waste any more time getting to know her. Obvious that all he was after was sex.

Good.

Please, don't let anybody I know see me with him!

Amy met clients at the Hyatt all the time, so her gaze scanned the people they saw as soon as she emerged from the revolving doors of the Hyatt on Steve's arm. Every woman they passed stared at Steve and then shot shy, envious smiles at Amy.

He was *that* good-looking. Not that he seemed to notice their admiring glances. At first Amy felt nervous, but gradually because of the other women, she began to cling a little harder to his arm. After all, at least for tonight, he was hers.

Amy had done quite a few events here. Like a lot of the Austin locals, she particularly loved this hotel. Its bar on the first floor had a Wild West decor, and it dominated the flashy lobby with views of Town Lake. Long-horns and cowboy boots adorned the walls as well as a gun rack filled with real BB guns.

Besides using the hotel as a venue, she sometimes met clients or caterers here after work. The comfortable couches and chairs were oversize and covered in brown-and-white cowhide. They were spaced widely enough apart so that other people couldn't eavesdrop on her meetings.

Tonight the walls of glass provided a dazzling view of downtown's glamorous skyline. Steve chose an out-side table on the huge patio overlooking the water and "Bat Bridge" and the hike-and-bike trail.

"Too bad we're too late to see the bats," she said.

The bats swarmed out of the Congress Avenue Bridge at dusk every evening much to the delight of their fans, who massed in the hundreds under the bridge to see them.

"If you've seen one bat, you've seen 'em all." Steve's big hand closed over hers.

She laughed. "I think there's something magical about them."

"Right. They eat mosquitoes."

She smiled.

"How come you looked so sad when you blew out the candle of your cake?" he asked after they'd sat in com-panionable silence in their shadowy corner for a while.

"It's my birthday."

"Oh, right. Your thirtieth. The birthday that makes all women crazy."

"I feel like life is passing me by."

"Then don't let it. Seize life." He stroked her hand while his unwavering gaze stirred her nerves until they felt taut.

"I know what you want."

She wasn't being fair, blaming him for the chemistry between them. But where was it written that a woman should be fair? Men took advantage, so why shouldn't she?

"I did seize life—once," she admitted, looking away, her eyes burning a little. "I...I made mistakes. I..." The shimmering lake seemed to blur.

It was an illusion, she told herself. She never cried.

She felt his fingers under her chin as he turned her vulnerable face back to his. "You look so unbearably sad all of a sudden. Why?"

"Sorry. I don't mean to be such a drag," she said.

"You're not. So, what happened?"

"Look—"

"I have ghosts, too," he said. "One was my older brother. Only, he finally straightened his life out."

"Who said anything about ghosts?"

"Well, something's damn sure eating you, darlin'. My number-two ghost is a gorgeous blonde."

"I'm blond."

"Exactly. You even look a little like her. In fact, when I first looked at you, you scared the hell out of me. So, we're both living dangerously tonight."

"What went wrong between you and her?"

"I suppose it's a common enough story," he said in an easy voice that didn't quite match the bleak emptiness in his eyes. "She left me for my best friend and business partner."

"Oh, that's rough. I'm sorry. When?"

"A year ago today."

"And you're not over her?"

"I tell myself I am."

"Where does she live?"

"Here. In Austin."

"Do you ever see her?"

"This morning, as a matter of fact." His face went dark and still.

"And if she changed her mind about you—"

"I tell myself I've learned my lesson, that I'd walk away. No! I'd run!"

"But would you?"

He didn't answer.

"You didn't run when you saw me, and you said I looked like her."

When he shoved his chair back, the metal legs grated on the rough concrete. "Can we talk about something else other than Madison?"

"Sure."

Madison. So that was her name. And since she lived here, she could be dangerous.

Only to the next woman who fell in love with him. Never to Amy, since they couldn't possibly have a future. Still, she swallowed tightly.

Amy didn't know what to say for a while, but it didn't seem to matter. She understood about inner demons. So they sat together in the darkness, and as it had been on the dance floor, she found it easier to be with him than she ever could have imagined. What did it matter if she was a stand-in for a woman he couldn't have?

"I'd rather talk about my ranch or my family than Madison," he said after a while.

"What's your family like?"

"I grew up in the east," he said. "I was a big-city boy. Manhattan. I have an older brother, Jack. He's forty and real serious, at least since—" When he stopped himself abruptly, she wondered why. "And a younger sister, Violet. She ran a little wild for a while, but now she's a doctor. Very respectable."

Amy shivered a little and glanced out at the lake, which looked like thick, glossy ink in the sparkling darkness.

"Go on," she said.

"I've got two more brothers—Miles and Clyde—same age as me."

"What?" She couldn't believe it. "So you're a—"

"Triplet."

She smiled. "And proud of it?"

"Sometimes—when they behave."

"So, are you all alike?"

"I'm supposed to be the smartest. Clyde's got the worst temper, and Miles can rib you until you want to sock him."

"Wow."

"We visited Texas as boys, and the land got into my blood. Jack wasn't much for Texas back then, but Clyde and Miles and I used to pretend we were cowboys and ride stick horses."

"So did I."

"When I graduated from college I moved to Texas and went into business with my college roommate, Larry Cabot."

"He's the one who ran off with Madison?"

Steve hissed through his teeth as he lifted his chin. "He had family money, and I had ambition. I was willing to work hard, too."

Smarts, she thought, feeling her chest swell in admiration as if his brains and success reflected on her somehow. Which was ridiculous. They weren't a couple.

"I started a bar and restaurant with him and began buying land with my brothers. But even though I ranched with them, I always wanted a place of my own. Times were hard for a while. The realities of ranching are different from fantasy. I thought having a ranch of my own was a dream I might never realize. Then when the Shiny Pony Bar and Grill became a success, Cabot and I bought the Lonesome Saloon."

His mouth thinned. "Today we signed papers that make him the sole owner of the Lonesome. I ended up with the Shiny Pony."

She lifted his hand with the blistered finger and kissed the red welt. "I saw you come out of the kitchen sucking this. No wonder you didn't want to make out at the Lonesome Saloon."

"Make out? Is that what we're going to do?"

She leaned closer and parted her lips. When she licked them, she tasted him. "I certainly hope so. But first tell me about this ranch you're so wild about."

"Like I said, my first venture was with my triplet brothers. We pooled our resources and went in together on a ranch we call Flying Aces. Then about five years ago, I decided to look for some land of my own. I shopped for months without buying so much as an acre. Then one night I was driving around lost on some endless county road and feeling discouraged when I happened onto a place that had belonged to the same family for generations. There was water, natural springs and a creek, cliffs, lots of grass and gorgeous old buildings. The house is nearly a hundred years old. It'll be something, really something, when I finish restoring it."

"You sound like you really love it."

"The old guy who owned it, Mel Foster, was in his late nineties. He loved it even more. His neighbor had been pestering him to sell to him for a decade. Only, he didn't much like his neighbor, and now that I know the guy, I can't blame him. Mel didn't much like his own wild-spending, urban nieces and nephews, either. He wanted someone who'd love the place like he did."

"And he chose you?"

"When I wandered up to his house he invited me to stay the night. We shared a meal in his stone cook shack and quite a few shots of whiskey that night. We talked about horses and cattle and land, about how we felt about it, about how dead I'd felt in New York all those years. The next morning we got up early. He pointed out his prize livestock, his best bulls, his longhorn cattle and the wild turkeys."

"It sounds like paradise."

Steve smiled at her. "I can't wait to show it to you."

"I can't wait to see—" She broke off. She would never see it. "Tell me more."

"Well, we got out of Mel's pickup and saw feral pigs in the thickets. There were plenty of white-tailed deer.

Quail, too. Then he showed me the bottom land as well as the incredible views from the dramatic cliffs. It was so beautiful. By noon I was in love. Come supper the ranch was mine. Mel lived there and took care of the place until he got sick. Then I took care of him."

"He's dead?"

Steve nodded, and she saw the sorrow in his eyes.

"He was like a third grandfather. I still miss him."

"I'm so sorry." She traced his knuckles with a fingertip.

"They did big write-ups on him in the Texas newspapers. He was a top-notch rancher and had won international awards, yet he lived simply in a bunkhouse with only a few personal items. He kept the big house in perfect shape, like a museum. Said it was too luxurious for him. All he cared about was working the ranch. I won't ever forget him."

"I know what's it's like to lose someone you'll never forget."

"I guess everybody does, darlin'. Mel was a big man. I want to make him proud…if he's looking down."

"I'm sure you will." She paused. "I…I used to spend a lot of time at a beautiful ranch that's probably near yours…with a friend," Amy whispered. "A long time ago. We liked to ride horses together."

"Is she dead, too?"

"She was in an accident." Amy wrapped her hand around his and held on tight. Then she swallowed and said no more. She felt the warmth of his eyes on her face, but she didn't dare look at him.

"I wish you'd tell me what's wrong," he said gently.

"Something's eating at you, and it's not going to stop unless you do something about it."

"I can't. I just can't."

"Not tonight maybe. But I'm here. I'll listen…when you're ready. I'll give you all my phone numbers."

He said it as if he was sure they had some sort of future.

But we don't. We just have tonight.

That truth made her heart ache even before he leaned forward and brushed his mouth softly across hers, his tongue teasing until she parted her lips.

His mouth was warm, and every time he licked or sucked or pressed his lips into hers even just a little, he sent shockwaves of pleasure throughout her body.

"You ready to get the hell out of here?" he muttered fiercely.

"Just one more kiss," she whispered against his mouth.

"One more for the road?" He laughed as his lips nuzzled the side of her throat. "Only if I get to pick the spot."

"The spot?"

"The spot where I get to kiss you, darlin'."

His dark eyes drifted lazily down her breasts to her belly, as if searching for exactly the right place that would give them both a buzz that would last until they reached his hotel. His gaze was disturbingly sensual when it lingered on that intimate place between her thighs.

"You're wearing black lace panties," he said.

"How'd you—" She gasped, reddening with shock. "No! Not there!"

He laughed. Swiftly before she could stop him, he

pulled her black spandex blouse lower, exposing more of her left breast. Then bending his dark head, he kissed the tiny *L* she'd had tattooed there nine years ago to match the *A* Lexie had had tattooed on herself two days before.

The tattoo, which had sent her perfect mother into orbit, had seemed like a lark at the time. Now it was a brand that burned all the way to her heart. It was like the scarlet letter on Hester Prynne's bodice, a constant reminder to Amy of her original sin.

Amy cried out in pure anguish, pushing at his shoulders, struggling to escape him. He was relentless. All too soon his lips and tongue bathed the tiny *L,* the symbol of her secret shame, with hot, wet kisses. The warm gliding of his tongue made it an erotic, joyous place that belonged to him and to her instead of to Lexie.

Caught up in her tempestuous excitement, Amy was soon driven by fresh desire. Gripping his head as his mouth washed the lush flesh with the healing balm of his sensual love, she moaned.

"I want you. I want you so much," she whispered in a raw, agonized tone. "How can this be happening?"

"Ready to get the hell out of here yet?" he muttered. "Or do you want me to pick another spot to kiss?"

"If you even talk about it, I'll be a molten puddle in two seconds." When she sprang from her chair so he wouldn't kiss her again, her legs were so wobbly, she had to clutch the table for support. "I'm going to hate myself tomorrow."

"No, you won't. I promise," he whispered, putting his arm around her waist. "Hold on to me."

"I'm afraid."

"Don't be," he murmured. "I'm not. And that's a switch."

In his eyes she saw a strange emotion, which vanished before she could read it.

Even so, she clung to him, burying her face against his broad chest for a long moment. Why, why she was acting as if he could protect her against all the demons? But, of course, he couldn't. She knew that.

Nobody could. Her demons lay within.

Four

Standing in his birthday suit with hot water streaming all over him should have relaxed him. Except, Steve's mind got creative on him as he stared at the glistening white tile walls.

Paranoid might be a better word than *creative*.

Sally was gone. He was sure of it. The mere thought made his heart feel heavy and leaden.

You've got it bad, Fortune.

When he turned off the water and slammed the shower door open, a blast of frigid air stopped him. He should never have told her the name of his hotel and then let her follow his truck in her own car. He should never have left Miss Jones in his living room alone while he showered.

Fear knotted Steve's stomach even as the cold air raised goose bumps on his dark flesh. When he heard a sound in the other room, his heart leaped with a keen excitement. Hurrying, he strode about the cold, functional hotel bathroom, not caring that he dripped water all over the tiles, not caring when he nearly stumbled on the wet floor that was as slippery as polished glass.

Despite the shower and the chill, just thinking about her had him hard again. He wanted to thrust himself inside her, to claim her in the most primitive way. He wanted to stay inside her forever.

If he was wrong and she was gone, he'd have to go back to Town Lake and jog for hours.

Grabbing a towel, he rubbed his hair down first and then his body. To relax, he forced himself to whistle again as he had in the shower. When he was done, he threw the towel down and was about to open the door that led to the bedroom, when he realized he didn't have a stitch on. He was that eager.

Hell. Should he dress again?

No. He grabbed the towel and wrapped it around his waist. Striding into the living room, all he saw was furniture—a couch, two chairs, two lamps and a few books.

Where the hell was she? He stood there for a long moment, inhaling her scent, which floated in the room like her ghost.

Violets, she'd said. Feeling a loss he didn't understand, he picked up one of the books on the couch and threw it so hard, it smashed a lamp to bits.

He should never have left her alone, but his conscience had forced him to give her one last chance to run. He hadn't wanted her here if she didn't want to be here. What a sap he was.

He flung his front door open and stared out into the dark, empty hall.

"Sally?" His hoarse voice sounded way too needy.

He was stomping back to his bedroom to find a pair of jogging shorts when he heard a little cry from the kitchen. Golden hair flying, she came running through that door, holding a photograph she'd taken off his fridge as well as his book on Greek gods. "Did you fall? Are you hurt?"

"You're still here," he whispered in amazement. He flushed as he remembered the lamp. "You're really here?"

"Of course, darlin'," she mocked, smiling impishly as she drew a lock of her hair back to expose an elfin ear.

"For God's sake, don't tease me now."

"Are you all right?"

"I knocked a lamp over…by accident."

"Did you cut yourself?"

"No."

"So, you're a reader? A philosopher even? Plato? Homer?"

"The ancient Greeks are pretty amazing," he said.

"I didn't know cowboys read."

"I'm the smart triplet, remember?"

"I'm impressed."

He moved toward her and seized her in his arms, kissing her mouth, then her throat, and then her breasts with a madness and a hunger he had never felt before. The thought that he'd nearly lost her inflamed his senses. Every kiss was a raw act of possession. His desire for her was beyond reason. Not that he wanted to think about it.

"I thought you were gone," he murmured.

"I thought about it…maybe just a little," she admitted. "It's what I should do."

"Do you always do what you should?"

"For a long time I have." She hesitated, stroking his wet hair. "That was sweet of you to let me think about it. I like that. I like it a lot. I also like it that you're into the ancient Greeks. I don't just want you. I think I like you, too."

"I don't *think*. I *know* I like you. Just like I know you're wrestling with something difficult. That's why I wanted to give you a chance to split. I don't want you to do this if—"

"Now you're the one who's thinking too much, cowboy."

Before his next heartbeat, she set down the picture— the one of him and his triplet brothers stomping grapes that summer they'd gone backpacking in Europe and he'd discovered Greece—on a table along with his book and began tracing his body with her fingertips, letting them run lightly down his abdomen to his navel and then lower until he was on fire for her to pleasure him.

She smelled so damned sweet. Violets.

He groaned when her fingers slipped inside his towel and caressed his naked skin. Then she unknotted the towel, and terry cloth swished down his legs and pooled on the floor. She knelt and placed her hands on the back of his bare legs. Heat shot through him when her lips neared his thighs. He felt her warm breath first, then her tongue. She licked him before her mouth took him whole.

He gasped even before she began moving her head.

She knew a lot. Too much. More than he wanted her to.

Definitely, she was no virgin. But then what had he expected from a single girl in revealing black spandex that cupped her breasts and butt? Hell, she'd had the first letter of some guy's name tattooed above her heart. If she were smart, she'd never tell him that story. He'd be tempted to hunt the guy down and punch him if he ever found out who he was.

Even as he tried to tell himself she was hot and wild and perfect for a one-night stand, the thought of bedding her and never seeing her again aroused some fierce, irrational possessiveness inside him. Swiftly he pressed her head more tightly against his groin. His feelings hacked at him like a dull machete, making a thousand little cuts that all bled for her. He couldn't bear to think of her with other men.

"Do you have a boyfriend?" he muttered thickly.

She jumped back and stood up. She couldn't possibly read his expression in the darkness since the only light came from the kitchen behind him.

"Do you?" he demanded in a low, harsh tone.

"No!" Her voice was indignant, furious even.

He was equally furious. "Well, you do now."

"You think you and I— No. I can't date you. And I can't explain why I can't, either, so don't ask. But it's not because I'm dating anyone else."

"I don't know what came over me," he muttered. And he didn't. "It's just that you make me feel things… I'm not accustomed to feeling at this stage in a…relationship."

"We can't have a relationship." Her wide-open eyes met

his equally stunned gaze. "But me, too," she admitted in a low voice that was a shade shy of a whisper. Her thin face, which was framed with wild golden hair, was white.

Hell. He'd scared her again with his attack of macho possessiveness.

"Darlin', darlin', it's okay."

She touched his cheek, traced the line of his mouth with a fingertip. Then her soft hand moved lovingly down his throat.

"What is it about you, huh?" he asked. Then to his surprise, he saw tears in her eyes.

"You're crying. Why?"

She touched her lashes and then her wet cheeks. "Oh, my. I am. I really am. I…I can't believe it. I haven't cried in… I can't believe it. I'm crying." She began to laugh a bit hysterically.

"What's wrong? What did I say?"

She clung to him and then laid her golden head against his heart where his pulse pounded so violently. "Just hold me. Just hold me." Her voice was low and choked. "Hold me until I'm myself again."

Her whole body began to shake. Hell, she was really going to cry. He hated tears. Most of all he hated himself for making her cry.

"Oh, Steve, I…I've wanted to cry for so long, and I just couldn't." Her words came out in fits and starts. "The pain was just too much."

"There, there," he murmured as she wept endlessly, her body racked with sobs. His chest was wet with the flood of tears as she continued to weep. "It's okay," he said, ruffling her hair and stroking her back.

His words seemed to make her cry harder.

"You don't understand. It'll never be okay."

"Short of murder, nothin's that bad."

"Murder," she sobbed, crying all the harder.

After that he said nothing until she quieted. Then he became aware of her body against his, aware that he was naked and that it wouldn't take much to pull her blouse and skirt off and get her naked, too.

He knew he should be noble and resist her when she pressed closer, seeking a different kind of comfort from him. But when she started kissing him on the chest and sucking at his nipples, he lowered his head to hers and kissed her hard on the mouth, his intentions clear. Without giving her a chance to change her mind, he pulled her blouse to her waist and ripped her skirt to her knees, which left her wearing her black lacy panties and her cowboy boots.

"No bra?" he murmured.

"Shelf bra."

Whatever that was.

"I'll take off the boots," she said.

"Leave them on," he whispered, tugging off her panties.

"Kinky."

"Not really." His hands began to roam her body freely. She was hot, lush satin and wet *there*. He kissed her again, rotating his hips against hers, forcing her to feel his erection as his lips and tongue caressed her everywhere. In no time her nipples were as hard as pebbles.

Then he picked her up and carried her to the closest wall. Pushing her against it, he wrapped her booted legs around his waist and was about to plunge inside her when she said, "No!"

"What?"

"We're forgetting…" She was too breathless to go on.

"What?"

"Condoms!"

"Right. Damn."

"Don't go anywhere," he whispered against her hair. "Don't you dare go anywhere."

She laughed and spread his towel on the floor and lay down on it while he raced around the hotel suite like a madman.

In two seconds he was back on the floor beside her, fumbling with the damn wrapper. Then he had it on, and he was inside her, where he belonged.

She was tight and hot…so hot.

He groaned. She pulled him closer with a gentle sigh. He kissed each darling ear.

Then he began to pump as she held on to him fiercely. She felt too good, because it was over in seconds, at least for him. Afterward as he held her, shame licked through him, even though it had felt wonderful. When he could breathe normally again, his eyes connected with hers through the darkness.

"Sorry," he muttered raggedly, touching his perspiring forehead to hers. "I…I don't know what happened. I've never…lost control like that before."

She stroked his cheek silently. "It was great."

"Next time…."

"Don't apologize. I loved being with you." She continued to trace the line of his jaw with the back of her hands with such tenderness his heart ached. What was it about her that made him feel so much so intensely so fast? They'd just had sex. He barely knew her, and he never wanted to let her go.

He grabbed her hand and wove his fingers through hers. "Sally," he murmured. "Sally." Then he kissed her fingers, one by one.

When he led her into the bedroom, he knelt on the floor while she sat on the bed. Together they removed her boots. Then he ripped off the spread and pulled back the covers, and they got into his bed, snuggling closer and closer until their bodies fit perfectly and they were spooning. Inside her or outside her, no woman had ever felt so right.

She began to caress him, and soon her featherlight fingertips tracing the length of his spine had him buzzing. When he reached for her, she pushed his arms gently down on the sheets.

"My turn. I…I want to be in control this time. It's very important to me."

He gazed at her across his pillow. Again he was aware of those ghosts haunting her.

"All right. Since you took off your boots."

She smiled. Then she began stroking the tip of his erection with her hand until he jumped every time she touched him, until he felt spirals of ever-hotter fire radiating throughout his body. Soon he was breathing hard and could think of nothing but burying himself inside her. Still those silky, warm fingers kept making those slow, erotic circles.

More than anything he wanted to grab her hand, to force her to squeeze him harder, to rush her.

But he didn't. Aw, hell. He thought surely he would die a thousand little deaths before she finally kissed him on the mouth and opened her lips. When finally she climbed on top of him and straddled him, he tore another plastic package open—as a tiny hint. When she took the condom from him and put it on him, it was all he could do not to lose control.

She laughed at his throaty moan and pushed her bottom down on top of him. Again she was tight and soft and warm and a perfect fit. When he started to pump, she splayed her hands against his chest and whispered, "No! My turn…"

He groaned.

"You promised."

"I'm dying here, darlin'."

"Oh no, you're not. You're very very much alive."

Then she began sliding slowly up and down on top of him, bouncing rhythmically, her own rhythm though, not his, and not quite at the speed he longed for, either.

Still, it was great. He liked her long golden hair brushing his throat and shoulders. He liked the way she was crooning to herself and the way she seemed to be enjoying herself so much she stretched these moments of ecstasy into a long, feverish, almost unendurable and yet ever-so-delicious agony for them both.

Finally the building pressure inside him was so fierce he had to close his eyes, clench his teeth and knot the sheets with his fists to wait for her. Somehow, and just barely, he hung on even when the desire for release lit every nerve in his male being. He felt like a bomb one instant before it detonated. She made second after second tick by—pulse beats of delicious wanting, wanting, wanting this gorgeous woman with an intensity that he'd never known before.

When the explosion came, it was mutual. She screamed and clung, and he damn sure embarrassed himself by doing the same.

Afterward, when she continued to clutch him, crying softly against his chest, he felt big and manly—protective. When their bodies cooled and he'd kissed away her tears, he couldn't bear the thought of letting her go. For a long time while she slept, he held her, staring at the ceiling.

Something cataclysmic had just happened in his life. Never before had he felt so utterly completed by a woman. Not even by Madison.

Not even close.

A great tenderness for the woman in his arms welled inside him. He knew without a trace of doubt that Sally was *the one*. Which was hellishly scary because he didn't even know her.

Damn it. He had sworn he would never trust his heart to a woman unworthy of it again. And here he was, in the grip of something way stronger than he should be with a virtual stranger. That was the trouble with life and with people. You thought you were in control. Wrong. You could be in deep water with the first awkward step in a relationship, and suddenly your life wasn't yours anymore.

In the morning he would start trying to win her trust. He had to find out why she'd cried and why that was a big deal. Even though he knew better than to try to rescue another person, what choice did he have?

He was in too deep. He couldn't fail with her as he had with Madison. He simply couldn't. Too much was at stake.

Snuggling closer into her sweet-smelling warmth, he knew he wanted to hold Sally like this every night for the rest of his life. He nuzzled the nape of her neck with his lips, and the mere softness of her skin stirred him. If he lost her, she'd take a real piece of him with her.

She was the one woman for him.

Yet somehow he knew—hell, he was the smart triplet, wasn't he?—that she spelled trouble.

When Amy awoke, naked, her long limbs tangled in Steve's, the icy bedroom was dark except for the gray edges of light around the tall, rectangular windows. Her breathing was slow and measured, relaxed. Her body was filled with indescribable warmth. For a long moment she lay there in a state of utter contentment. As her hands moved across the sheets, she realized she'd never known such a profound sense of tranquillity. Then her hand brushed a warm, muscular arm, and she realized where she was and whose arms wrapped her. For a long moment she let herself sink into the tranquil bliss of just being with him, and in those brief seconds before her brain took over, she felt like a flower blossoming in a paradise that was eternal spring.

Then logic kicked in. It was morning. She had a job, and she'd probably overslept. There were probably a dozen messages on her cell phone and more on her office voice mail. She had calls to make, caterers to meet, hoteliers to woo, budgets to fine tune, and her major client to suck up to.

Her next breath was quick and shallow.

"Steve. Oh, my God."

Her temple pounded painfully. She had an awful headache. The soft tissues between her legs ached, too. He was big and he'd been an enthusiastic lover. She was sore down there, which meant she'd think of him all day.

Even now she wanted to forget about her cell phone messages. She wanted to stroke his hair, to kiss his throat and his mouth, to kiss him awake and then make love to him for hours.

Frowning, she forced herself to focus on her early meeting with her favorite caterer. Last thing yesterday her number-one client had told her he never wanted to use the caterer again. Amy still didn't know how she was going to explain. Also, sometime today she had to call her mother. But first she had to get out of here without waking Steve up. He made her feel things and want things. That terrified her.

Still, for another endless moment she lingered in his warm embrace and felt sad that she had to leave him. He was sweet. He'd been incredible in bed, too. So incredible she wished her life were different…she wished she were different.

She wished she deserved him. She wished she was the kind of person who didn't disappoint those she loved most.

Careful not to awaken him, she shifted a little.

Oh my, she *was* sore. Gingerly, inch by painful inch, she scooted her tender body away from his.

She grabbed her boots on the way to the living room where she found her panties, skirt and blouse. Quickly she dressed. She'd only managed to pull one boot on, when she heard something crash in the bedroom.

Another lamp? Was he coming after her like a big bear on the rampage the way he had last night?

"Sally!" His voice was a roar.

With a smothered little cry, Amy grabbed her other boot and purse and ran. On her way out the door, the boot caught on the doorknob and went flying back into his living room.

The bedroom door slammed open and he yelled for somebody named Sally again.

Sally? Who was Sally, Amy wondered as she quickened her step.

Then she remembered that she'd told him her name was Sally.

That was good. At least he would never be able to find her or tempt her again.

Five

Steve woke up with a queasy feeling in his stomach and knew something was vitally wrong. No longer did he feel the silken coils of his lover's golden hair caressing his shoulder. No longer did he inhale the sweetness of violets with every breath. No longer did her soft, sweet arms wrap him.

He sprang into a sitting position and instantly regretted it.

She was gone.

Gray rectangles of light spun sickeningly, causing his empty stomach to roil. Last night he hadn't eaten, preferring beer to the pizza he'd ordered. Now his eyelids burned and his brain felt foggy. Still, when he heard his front door close, his heart leaped. He hurled himself out of bed. Dragging a sheet, he stumbled into the living room, shouting her name.

His front door was open. As he ran through his living room, he tripped over something and fell forward into the dimly lit hall. He was picking up a black boot with little embroidered red roses when Mr. Beezee, the man who had the room across from his, opened his door and knelt to get his paper. Beezee's gray hair was neatly combed. Even his blue-and-white striped robe looked pressed and starched.

"Good morning," Steve muttered grumpily, forgetting he was unshaven and holding an ill-fitting sheet wrapped around his waist.

His neighbor's jaw gaped open and he stared at Steve as if he was the devil incarnate. Seizing his newspaper, Beezee banged his door shut.

When Steve shut his own door, his pulse hammered more painfully than ever. Hell. The last thing he needed before his meeting with the governor was trouble with Beezee again or a call from the hotel management evicting him for indecent exposure.

The governor! Breakfast!

Steve glanced at his watch and then at the high-heeled black boot. The boot was hand stitched and fashioned of the finest leather. It had to be custom-made and expensive. Two thousand dollars easy.

Cinderella—or rather Sally Jones—shouldn't be that hard to track down. Not for a modern-day prince who prided himself on his smarts.

If you're so damned smart, you'd have picked a brunette.

A few phone calls to pricey boot makers, and he'd have Miss Jones's address and phone number.

But first—the governor.

If Steve hurried, he'd be ten minutes late. Not an option. Tom Meyers didn't like to wait. He was the busy and commanding sort who kept other people waiting.

On his way to the bathroom, Steve tossed the boot onto his couch.

Later.

When Amy stepped out of her shower, she still felt tender from all the lovemaking. As she was rustling through hangers of clothes in her closet to find something to wear, Amy's landlord's dog started barking.

Amy smiled. What was it this time—a bug or a leaf? Whatever it was, Cheryl's wussy teacup poodle, Sparky, sounded every bit as ferocious as a bulldog, which was what Cheryl had meant to buy when they'd gone to the breeder. But her spoiled daughter, Kate, had fallen for Sparky, who was a bit of a nuisance, to say the least.

Cheryl owned an immense limestone mansion in one of the plushest neighborhoods in central Austin. She was also, as luck would have it, one of Austin's richest and most eligible bachelorettes.

Amy's mother, who was a social climber par excellence, had run into Cheryl at an art gathering right after her divorce and had arranged for Amy to rent the apartment over Cheryl's garage, which had been built as maid's quarters.

Amy could just hear her bossy, persuasive mother using her courtroom tactics on Cheryl.

"You and your daughter all alone in that big house? You don't need a live-in. You need more security. Now, if my daughter, who's looking for a place, were to rent your little apartment…"

It hadn't hurt that Cheryl and Amy used the same gym and were in the same spin class. Nor that they actually liked each other.

It was so important to Amy's mother that Amy live in such a neighborhood on a fifteen-million-dollar property she could brag about to her law partners that, to shut her up, Amy had finally moved out of an apartment she had loved.

"How can you prefer your apartment to this?" her mother had demanded when she'd driven her by Cheryl's for the tenth time. "Nobody at your apartment complex is *anybody*."

"I don't care. I don't hang out with them, anyway."

"My point exactly! Cheryl was married to that computer zillionaire. She's exactly the kind of connection you need to get your life on track."

"But—"

"You've been moping ever since college. Be nice to her and maybe she'll introduce you to someone, dear."

"'Someone' being a man?"

Her mother had dropped by the apartment with a hanging ivy right after Amy had finally rented it and moved in. Amy had been painting the apartment walls the color of golden honey.

"You should have gone with white," her mother had said.

"I like this color."

Her mother, who was black-haired, tall and reed thin, had pursed her lips. Not that she'd overruled Amy's opinion. Instead she'd moved about the apartment, her intense, burning black eyes, taking in everything. Finally she'd paused by a window and after a lengthy study of Cheryl's mansion and the pool, she'd given Amy *the* look.

"You'll meet our kind of people here."

"Cheryl's way older than me, Mother."

Her mother's brows had arched wickedly. "She doesn't look it."

"Ouch."

Like a lot of really rich women, Cheryl did whatever it took to stay young looking. Her present lover was even younger than Amy.

"She certainly married well, didn't she?" her mother said in her sweetie-sweet tone as she continued to look out at the pool, studying the imported Italian lawn furniture, the fountains, the red canopies and the lush landscaping.

"He divorced her."

"Which means she has his money and doesn't have to put up with him."

"That's marrying well?"

"You missed a spot, dear."

Amy raised her paintbrush and swiped the place her mother was pointing at.

"The next best thing to marrying well is divorcing well," her mother said. "She's got money, a cute lover, a fabulous house and she looks great. Take notes, dear."

Amy loved Cheryl now and her blue-haired daughter, Kate, but not because she saw them as connections.

They were just a mother and daughter with way too much money, who were struggling with all sorts of issues. For one thing, Kate's rich father wanted nothing to do with either one of them. To get his attention Kate constantly rebelled. She chose friends "normal" kids considered weird, wore rags and dyed her hair every color of the rainbow. Right now it was a startling neon blue. Not that her daddy had even noticed.

Amy knew all about rebellion, about fathers never noticing. Except, her rebellion had been caused by her mother's tyranny, not her father's benign neglect. She'd wanted her parents' approval more than anything, so her rebellion had been a secret thing, like a deadly drug that had destroyed her and her parents. Not just them. Lexie, too.

She'd been a happy kid before adolescence. Her mother hadn't known what to do with small kids, so she'd been raised by her father and kindly nannies. It was only when Amy had turned thirteen that her super-compulsive mother had suddenly taken a much more active role, picking her friends with the attention of a dictator choosing his generals, because the choices Amy made even at that early age could affect her future.

When Amy had argued, her mother had dominated and crushed Amy's independent spirit by grounding her and making her a virtual prisoner. Slowly a deep anger to be something other than the successful, well-dressed, popular robot her mother approved of had begun to burn inside Amy. When she'd gone to her father at sixteen and pleaded for the freedom to date a certain cowboy, he'd said her mother was in charge. Her mother had even wanted her to stop riding.

Amy had felt if she didn't do something, her mother would destroy everything she was. So she'd started playing the dutiful daughter, coming home at the right hours, appearing to run with her mother's choices of friends, making good grades, but all the while she'd been sneaking out. And so had Lexie.

Amy went to her mirror and pulled her long blond hair back into a ponytail. This morning there was no trace of that rebellious young girl. Her face was lightly made up. She looked very professional in cream-colored slacks and a matching long-sleeved silk blouse that she'd buttoned all the way to her throat. She wore no jewelry, and her beige pumps were low and sensible.

Not that beige was her color, but then, that was why she wore it. Unlike her mother, who always, even when she was in the courtroom, dressed with dramatic flair, Amy didn't want to look flashy or stand out in any way.

Never again!

Except for last night.

Unbidden came a vision of herself in Rasa's low-cut black spandex. She shivered at the jolt of heat she felt even as she remembered Steve mouthing the little *L* on her left breast outside the Hyatt. He'd thought she was a bad girl for sure.

She felt hot. In spite of her best intentions, a smile tugged at the corners of her mouth. Then she lifted her chin up and told herself that the new, reformed Amy would not think about him—ever again.

On her way to the door, the reformed Amy grabbed her briefcase and purse and her cup of coffee, but just as she touched the doorknob, a timid hand tapped lightly on the other side of her door.

Had Steve followed her somehow? Her heart thumped eagerly until she raised her shade and saw that it was her father. She laughed because in his black spandex shorts, fluorescent-red riding shirt, mirrored sunglasses and skull-shaped black bicycle helmet, he looked like an alien from another planet.

She threw the door open. "Daddy!"

Mike Sinclair handed her a small silver-wrapped box with a white bow on it.

"This is a treat, Daddy. You never come by without Mother."

He shrugged sheepishly. "Happy birthday, sweetheart."

She pulled at the white bow on her present. "This is for me?" she whispered. "From you?"

"I hoped I'd catch you before you left for work. Usually you're gone when I come by."

"You've come by before?"

His quick nod both thrilled and surprised her.

"I had no idea."

"I've been worrying about you more and more."

"You have?"

He nodded.

"I'm fine, Daddy."

"You always say that. Because you're like me. Because you want to believe it. You think if you just keep on keeping on, things will work out."

What did that mean, she wondered. Was he unhappy?

"Sometimes you have to do something…to change…." He stopped. "But who am I to give advice?"

Suddenly she wished he wasn't wearing those mirrored sunglasses so she could read his eyes. He shifted as if he suddenly felt uncomfortable. "I'm probably keeping you—"

"No."

Her father was an exercise addict. He biked or jogged for miles every morning before he went into his office to pull teeth, build bridges and preach dental hygiene to the hordes in need of conversion to daily flossing. Exercise time was the only time he had for himself. Luckily Mother approved of exercise.

He turned. "I've got ten more miles to—"

"Don't you want to see me open your present?" Like a greedy child she tore the paper off, gasping when she discovered an exquisite miniature silver horse wrapped in tissue.

She fingered the fine workmanship of the gleaming figurine. "Why, it's beautiful, Daddy! How sweet of you to remember."

He pulled his mirrored sunglasses off, studying her face too intently. Usually he was her absentminded father. Today his kindly blue eyes burned with fierce protective pride, just as they had the day he'd finally taught her to parallel park.

"You used to give me a horse on every birthday when I was younger."

"Until your mother said the last thing you needed was more horses."

"I...I could never have enough little horses. Not if they were gifts you picked out."

"When you were a little girl, it was so easy to love you." He hesitated. "I've missed you."

"I know." The gift and his saying those words made her long for that innocent time before she'd become a teenager, when she'd been so sure of her parents' love and pride in her, especially his. But life marches on. She was an adult now. And she'd disappointed them. There was no going back.

"It's just that I'm so busy," she said.

"You're just like your mother in that way."

His words stung.

"I...I'd rather be like you."

"Your mother's a whirlwind, a real mover and a shaker."

"You're as easygoing as she is uptight."

"I used to be. She keeps me moving," he continued. "That's for sure. She puts a weekly calendar on the fridge. If I don't look at it every morning, I can get into lots of trouble. But enough about your mother."

Amy sighed in relief.

"I'd better let you get to work."

"Thanks for coming by, Daddy."

He backed down the steps. She glanced at the little horse one last time before rewrapping it in tissue and setting the box on her kitchen windowsill. By the time she'd closed her door and dashed down the stairs, he was a lone figure biking down the trail into the woods of Pease Park.

Sometime today she had to call Mother. As always, Amy dreaded her mother's critical questions and demands.

Amy stared out at the sparkling turquoise pool. What was Steve doing right this moment? If only she had the right to call him and find out.

What was his life like? Who was he really? Her chest tightened. What did he care about? What were his quirks? His passions? She swallowed against a sudden lump in her throat and was surprised how much it hurt that she would never know.

When she reached her Toyota, a hot wind blew through the trees and made her ponytail flutter against her nape. She remembered Steve's burning mouth there. Memories of his mouth, hot and seeking in even more intimate places, made her tender pelvis ache. How was she ever going to get through her day if she kept thinking about last night?

Steve was only five minutes late to the governor's office; however, Tom kept him waiting because he'd had to fit an important state senator into his schedule before their breakfast meeting.

"Crisis about school funding," his secretary had said rather wearily as she'd handed Steve coffee. "But you're lucky. The later it is in his day, the farther behind he runs."

While Steve sipped black coffee in the waiting room, he thought about Miss Sally Jones. Strangely, he kept remembering her haunted blue eyes more than he did the red-hot sex. Which meant if he really were the smart triplet, he'd forget about playing detective. He was probably lucky as hell she'd run.

Rescuing damsels in distress was a bad habit of his. You couldn't save people. He knew that from Jack and

Madison. People had to save themselves. When a man tried to save a woman and failed, the woman usually repaid him by hating him for having gotten her hopes up.

At least, Madison had.

Okay, you got off easy this time. You had a night of uncomplicated sex.

Like hell.

He wanted her again.

Was he a wimp or what? Women were supposed to feel romantic after sex. Not men.

He wanted her again.

He got up and asked the secretary for the yellow pages. Opening the thick book, he flipped pages until he landed on boot makers.

Don't even think about jotting a number down.

He scribbled a few names and numbers just for the hell of it. Not that he was about to call any of them. He was still trying to talk himself out of calling as he reached for his cell phone.

Hell.

She'd run out on him. If it was that easy for her to walk out, he should forget her. He wadded up the paper with the boot makers' numbers, got up and stalked to the trash can.

It was hard to walk back to his chair without that crumpled ball of paper, but he was through being a self-destructive sap who thought he could save people.

No more Madisons!

No more Sallys!

It was high time he remembered he was the smart triplet and started acting the part.

But what if she needed him? Really needed him to—

He leaned forward and breathed deeply. Then he clenched his hands and raked through his dark hair. Again he thought about those phone numbers in the trash can.

Somehow he stayed put in his chair.

Breakfast with the governor was in a tacky back room at a little taqueria on Congress Avenue. Tom was a big bear of a man with a voracious appetite, at least where food was concerned. He was addicted to these particular taquitos.

"I have to have at least one a week," Tom had said during their short, brisk walk to the taqueria. The governor had glad-handed every stranger he met on the sidewalk, even the homeless beggars. His security men had followed them like a pack of nervous guard dogs.

One taquito—hell! Tom had gulped down four already.

Steve shoved his empty plate aside. After eating three of the giant taquitos smothered in hot sauce the governor had ordered for him, Steve felt too full and wished he'd reined in a little.

Meanwhile Tom was still firing questions at him in between bites, demanding details about the layout of the Loma Vista Ranch where the Hensley-Robinson Awards Banquet to honor Ryan Fortune for his charitable works on environmental issues was to be held come next November.

"Since my office is sponsoring this event to honor Ryan, it has to go off without a hitch," Tom said, wiping his lips with a napkin. "We'll have a lot of high-profile guests. My reputation is at stake. You can't be too care-ful about security these days, either. Not to mention No-vember is election month. I have enemies. Lots of them."

"I have a meeting with Ryan and Lily at the ranch around eleven if you're free today to see the place for yourself," Steve said.

"Short notice. Probably can't make it," Tom said brusquely. "Overcommitted on talking to people about this school-funding issue. Not that it matters. I pay for eyes and ears and brains, too." He grabbed his cell phone. "What if I send my events planner out today? She can report back to me with the answers to all my questions. I'll send along some security people, as well."

Before Steve could say it didn't have to be today, Tom was on the phone barking at the obviously over-worked, overpressured Burke so vigorously Steve al-most felt sorry for her.

Odd name for a woman, Steve thought, imagining a tough, masculine, schoolteacher type. Who else could handle Tom full-time?

"So, cancel your meetings," Tom growled when Burke apparently balked at being ordered to be at the ranch by eleven.

Tom was silent for a brief moment, a deep crease wrinkling his brow as he pretended to listen. "Look," he interrupted. "Just tell the hotel people they can take us or stay empty." Burke must have put up some sort of fight because Tom paused again. "How many times do I have to tell you? The hotel industry is a high fixed-cost business. They need us more than we need them."

Again Tom fell into a state of sullen agitation while

she must have tried to explain something. "Just do it," he ordered impatiently. His big face grew animated again. "Great. Great. Okay. Now that that's settled, your next priority *today* is to do what I just told you to do. Get out to Steve Fortune's Loma Vista Ranch."

He hesitated. "Yes, I said *Steve*. Have you met him or something?" Again there was a pause. "Okay, then. Get there with all my best security people by eleven o'clock sharp."

When she interrupted Tom again, he shook his head, really frowning this time. "I don't care how difficult it is. Just do your job and make the arrangements, so I can do mine." His voice was cold. "My secretary will fax yours a map to his ranch along with directions." He hung up without bothering to say goodbye.

"I could meet with her another time if it's inconvenient for her," Steve offered. "Give me her number."

"No. Draw me a map," Tom said almost curtly. "She'll be there. I want her feedback today." Tom's blue eyes sparked, but he smiled genially as he whipped a pen out of his shirt pocket and began to scribble on a notepad.

"I'm not always so tough on Burke. It's just that lately she's seemed distracted, especially today. Burke's only a few years older than my daughter, Lanie, but she's sensible. To tell the truth, Lanie's still a little wild."

Wild. Wildness was warmth flooding your entire body when you tasted violets as you licked a soft, molten breast tattooed with the letter *L*.

"Any tattoos?" Steve muttered gloomily.

"What? Tattoos?"

"Nothing," Steve said quickly, willing Sally to leave him the hell alone.

"Tattoos?" Tom said. "Burke?" He burst out laughing.

"She's thirty—going on sixty. Thirty yesterday as a matter of fact. I don't think she's taking it too well."

An alarm bell went off in Steve's brain.

Thirty yesterday... Like Sally.

The coincidence struck an odd note with him.

"You'll never meet a straighter, duller type than Burke," Tom said. "Not that I'm complaining. She's efficient and organized. Smart, too. Like her mother, who's an old friend of mine and major fund-raiser for the party. Carole's a high-powered trial attorney. Burke comes to work when I call her, no matter what the hour. Doesn't mind me calling her at any time of the day or night, either. She's the perfect gopher."

"Does she have a life?"

"She says she doesn't want one."

"Did you ever ask her why?"

"Why? I like it that she lives to serve me."

"Boyfriends?" Why the hell had he asked that?

"Burke lives like a nun. I'm not saying she couldn't be attractive—if she tried."

Steve thought of Sally, who'd said she didn't date, either.

"I can't wait to meet her," Steve said. "Eleven o'clock sharp."

"You'll be impressed. With her in charge, the Hensley-Robinson Awards Banquet will go off without a hitch."

"An events-planner robot."

Tom's automatic grin froze as he focused on Steve's dark face. "You know, kid, you're single. So is Burke. You could do worse. A whole lot worse. Burke comes from important people. But, hell, on second thought, stay away from her. I'd be tempted to hack the privates off any man who stole her from me."

"Don't worry. I'm already in love with somebody else." Steve stared at the governor in shock. "Forget I said that."

"Sure." He grinned.

As Steve raised his hand to signal for the check, a longing for Sally that verged on pain surged through him.

When the waiter brought the check, he grabbed it and bolted from his chair. He had to find Sally.

But later.

First he had to deal with Burke.

Six

So where was the paragon?

Steve's gaze wandered from the barn to the outbuildings as he held the screen door open. His ranch was crawling with Burke's people—caterers, entertainers, decorators, security guys and electricians.

But no Burke.

"Do we have a contingency plan, just in case you don't finish with construction?" Ryan Fortune asked, interrupting Steve's thoughts as he and Lily stepped out onto the warm, sun-dappled porch of Steve's ranch house and stood beside the new rust-colored King Ranch rockers.

The trouble was he'd been renovating the house for Madison. When she'd jilted him, he'd fired the best contractor in the county. Later, when he'd decided to go ahead with the project, he hadn't been able to get anybody but James, who liked to hunt and fish more than he liked to build.

"There've been delays, but it'll be done in time." Swearing under his breath when he saw Burke's people running in all directions, Steve led Ryan and Lily down the sidewalk. He'd just given them a tour of the house.

Now that they were outside, the light and the heat were enough to melt one's bones.

"Mel would approve of what you've done. The house is lovely," Lily said, turning back to look at it as she clutched Ryan's arm when they paused in the shade beneath a canopy of mesquite trees. "Really lovely. Authentic. Perfect. Madison—"

"It will be perfect," Steve said, interrupting her.

He stared at the two-story limestone mansion with its wraparound porches, his broad chest swelling with pride and happiness, not caring in the least that Madison was out of the picture even though they'd begun the remodeling together, thinking they'd live in it after they were married.

"It's so sweet of you to host the Hensley-Robinson Awards Banquet. It means so much to Ryan that you—"

"Don't mention it. Ryan's done more for me than I can ever repay. He's like a second father."

Ryan smiled at him fondly and then at Lily, whose dark eyes glowed with love. They looked good together, Steve thought. Like a lot of the local community, he was glad they'd finally found each other again.

They'd fallen in love as kids but had been cruelly separated. They'd both had earlier marriages. Now they couldn't seem to stop touching each other or watching each other. It was almost as if they were both afraid to let the other out of their sight for fear they'd lose each other again. Steve's gut twisted as he thought of Sally. He wanted that kind of deep, enduring love, too.

Hand in hand, the Fortunes walked ahead of him toward the barn. They were both dark and tall and still incredibly handsome. Their hair hadn't grayed even though they were nearly sixty. Ryan had worked the land all his life, and it showed. He was tanned and muscular and moved with a quick, light step despite the heat.

Lily, who had started off as the Fortunes' hired help, was still slim and voluptuous. Looking at her today, nobody would ever guess that this regal woman in white silk slacks and the crisp white blouse had ever been a maid. She had high cheekbones, and her glossy black hair was swept back from her face in a sleek twist. She'd come a long way from the days when she'd scrubbed linoleum floors on her knees.

Steve's gaze drifted past them, and he scanned the oak trees and rocky terrain that shimmered in the mid-morning heat for any sign of the events planner or James, his good-ol'-boy contractor or his workers. The carpenters, masons and painters were gone, and so were their trucks with those annoying bumper stickers that read, I'd Rather Be Fishing. Early lunch again, Steve supposed. He sure as hell hoped they didn't take a siesta or go fishing all afternoon. Hell, why couldn't they bring sandwiches?

At least the governor's security guys had shown up on time, so Tom would have his answers. Steve had counted six so far. They wore black slacks and white T-shirts and were swarming all over the house and grounds.

Striding over to one of the security guys who was filming the outside of his mansion with a video camera, Steve held out his hand and introduced himself. The man, who had sandy hair, friendly blue eyes and a muscular body, gripped his hand and shook vigorously.

"Randy Freeman."

"Steve Fortune." Steve hesitated. "So where's Burke?"

"You mean Amy?"

"The governor's events planner?"

"One and the same. Amy Burke-Sinclair. She gave me a ride here. Asked me to drive 'cause she had lots of calls to make."

"So, where is she?"

"I last saw her in the cook house. She's around here somewhere."

"Then why the hell hasn't she introduced herself?"

"She's catching hell because the governor canceled an event at the last moment. The hotel people are threatening massive penalties, and her job is on the line with the agency she works for. But, hey, if I see her, I'll sure tell her you're looking for her."

Randy smiled and then lifted his camera and began to shoot again.

Ryan and Lily were talking to two security men under an oak tree. Steven looked past them and saw from behind a young, nondescript blonde carrying a briefcase and a cell phone. Her ponytail bounced as she sashayed, and that was definitely the word for the way her cute behind bounced as she damn near galloped into his barn.

On second thought, at least from the back, she didn't look dull. Despite vanilla-colored slacks and a long-sleeved blouse, which covered her from chin to toe, she had a spectacular figure. At least he thought so. Her cell phone must have rung because she lifted it to her ear.

"Burke," he yelled.

In fact, hers was a seriously cute butt.

Damn it, if there wasn't something familiar about that behind.

Something damnably familiar…

Steve. Oh, God! Steve Fortune *is* my Steve.

Not *my* Steve, she thought, mentally correcting herself as she glanced warily up at the sky. What were the chances of something like this happening?

Less than a lightning bolt striking her out of that clear, blue sky. Was somebody up there out to get her?

Amy's heart was thudding violently as she fought to concentrate on the hotel manager's scathing denunciations while ducking behind an oak tree to hide from Steve.

Julio, the hotelier, was even more furious than her favorite caterer had been, and she didn't blame him. Due to budget problems and Tom's decision, she'd been forced to cancel Julio, and there was nothing she could do now but damage control.

Poor guy. The reason she always used him was that he worked so hard. She would have to send him a note as well as a little gift.

She hated confrontations, and she dreaded facing Steve after last night. How were they going to work together after…

Racing into the barn to get herself together, she inhaled the sweet odors of hay and leather and oats. Her footsteps rang on the concrete, scaring two swallows into swooping down at her from the rafters.

Protecting their nest probably, she thought, forgetting her conversation with Steve. A skinny yellow barn cat that had been napping on a sack of pellets sat up and arched his back. His slitted yellow eyes never left her as he curled his wiry, bottlebrush tail underneath him and settled back down to nap in the shadows again.

Instantly the suffocating heat and the sights and smells took her back to other barns and to Lexie. Oh, how they'd laughed together as they'd raced to grab bridles and blankets off the wall and tack up their horses. Her eyes misted.

Don't remember. It hurts too much. Even if Lexie was alive, you can't ever be that foolish, brave, loving girl again.

Hugging her briefcase against her chest, Amy closed her eyes for a long moment. Then she opened them. She had to focus on the disaster at hand.

Of all the bad luck! Steven Fortune was *her* Steve. She'd nearly fainted when she'd seen him walk out of his ranch house with Ryan Fortune. When she placed a hand over her left breast, her heart slammed into it. She had to calm down and figure out a way to act professionally before she faced him.

When a horse stomped and neighed impatiently from

one of the stalls, Amy was drawn to the familiar sound. Tiptoeing up to the stall, she found a gorgeous black horse stomping about on a bed of pine shavings.

The filly had a lot of Arabian blood in her. Good blood. Egyptian probably. Amy gazed into her wise, somber eyes and was immediately comforted by the horse's silent, eloquent message.

More than anything Amy wanted to unlatch the door and go inside and stroke the large darling until she felt strong enough to face Steve and the hotel people again.

"Sally?" Steve's deep voice was low and hoarse.

Amy jerked at the sound of that name. So, he'd recognized her, too.

Off to her right she saw a tall ladder leading to the loft. If she climbed it, maybe he would think she'd gone out the back way or he might simply give up his search and she'd have a few minutes to pull her thoughts together.

As she rushed through the sweltering darkness toward it, Amy thought she heard the *chop-chop* of helicopter rotors outside. Tom?

Tom had said he'd try to come, if he could get free, which was the last thing she needed after her nightmarish morning. The governor was decisive about big matters, but when it came to planning meetings and events he wasn't. He always demanded the best of everything in the beginning stages before contracts were signed. Then, when she had people hired, contracts signed and a workable budget, he'd say the costs were too high, bark a few orders and snap the rug out from under her, and she'd have to start over.

Stuffing her phone and purse into her briefcase, she scrambled up the ladder to the loft.

"Sally?"

The sound of that deep voice cut off Amy's breath as she crouched low against the wall of his barn.

"Sally?" he repeated. "I mean Burke or Amy," Steve muttered, sounding even more confused than she felt.

Go away. Leave me alone. Too much is happening too fast.

When he walked past the Arabian, the filly nickered to him, too. His heavy footsteps paused.

"Hi there, Noche. How are you doing, girl? How's the leg? Feeling any better? Had any visitors lately? Strangers?"

He left the horse then and stalked over to the ladder. "Miss Burke? If you're up there, come down. We've got a lot to discuss."

How could he sound so perfectly reasonable when this situation was so crazy?

Even when she heard his boot on the first rung of the ladder, she didn't cry out. She kept thinking maybe she could put this off until she was stronger.

Her mouth went dry as she remembered him stripping her and then holding her against his living room wall, her booted legs wrapped around his lean waist. He'd been so wild, she was still sore.

The higher he climbed, the lower she hunkered behind the hay bales. Even if he came up here, maybe he wouldn't see her.

When he sprang as quietly as a large cat onto the floor of the loft, she could almost feel his eyes seeking her in the scorching darkness.

"Miss Burke, I know you're up here," he said softly. "Because there's nowhere else you could be. What I don't know is why you're hiding. This is crazy. It's hotter than Hades up here."

Beads of salty perspiration dripped into her eyes and she wiped her brow.

"I don't know about you, but I'm sweating like a pig," he said.

She bit her tongue to keep from lashing out that pigs didn't sweat. He was right about it being hot, though. There wasn't a breath of air in the loft. Her hair was wet, and sticky moisture was trickling down her breasts. Five minutes more of this and she'd look like she'd been swimming in her vanilla silk pants.

Her fingers tightened around the handle of her briefcase. Slowly she got up off the floor, held her chin at a proud angle and walked up to Steve, who loomed over her. Standing in a ray of brilliance that sifted down from a high window, he blocked the only way down.

"So, it *is* you," he said, his eyes lighting with fires that burned her. "I was going to call every boot maker in Texas. This has to be a sign, darlin'."

"Maybe for you."

"Right." That sudden light in his eyes that connected them went out. He swallowed hard as if something in his throat refused to go down.

Still, no matter what, she couldn't encourage him. Pretending an indifference she was far from feeling, she drew a deep breath and fanned herself with her hand.

If the heat was bothering him, he didn't let on. In a crisp

white work shirt and starched jeans, he seemed taller and even more broad-shouldered than she remembered.

"You don't give up, do you?" she muttered.

"So, you gave me a false name last night?" His voice was smooth, but the brief flash of hurt in his dark eyes made her wince.

"Because I was serious about never wanting to see you again."

"Top of the morning to you, too, darlin'." Then his dark eyes glanced past her as if it hurt him too much to look at her.

"Don't tease," she whispered, feeling agonized, which was ridiculous.

"Who's teasing?" An impenetrable mask concealed his true emotions. Even so, the suppressed edge of passion in his low voice cut her. "My memories of you are apparently fonder than yours are of me. Hell, I saw your cute butt and ran to find you."

"Just what I want to think of as my most memorable quality."

His sudden grin made the air go out of her lungs.

"I haven't been able to forget you, you know," he muttered gloomily.

"It's only been a few hours."

"You know what I mean."

Scant inches separated their bodies. She wanted so much to touch him, to apologize. She ached with needs she didn't want.

"Quite a coincidence…you being Burke," he finally muttered.

"I prefer to call it rotten luck."

"I prefer black clingy silk and spandex." His low voice was charged, even though she could tell he was fighting to appear indifferent.

"I returned that skirt and top to Rasa," she whispered.

"You left one of your boots behind, Cinderella. That hers, too?"

"They were a gift from my father."

"So, what's with the bun and the shirt buttoned tight enough to strangle you?"

"I told you I wasn't the kind of girl you thought I was."

"I say actions speak louder than words." He chuckled.

Each breath she drew was so swift and hot her lungs burned even as her heart ached. "Last night wasn't the real me."

"I don't have a problem with sexy, complicated women." Steve held out his hand to guide her down the ladder.

When his fingers grazed hers, she jumped back, her breath coming faster. "Don't touch me."

"Easy," he muttered, that expressionless mask stealing over his features again.

She sighed, sensing she'd hurt him again.

Good. Maybe he'd leave her alone, she thought. And yet her heart ached.

"Last time I heard, sex between consenting adults wasn't a crime. I don't think you're a bad girl, if that's what you're so worried about—despite your tattoo."

"Don't you dare tell anybody—"

"Your secret is safe with me."

"Why don't I feel reassured?"

"So you're not Sally Jones? So what?"

"I'm Amy Burke-Sinclair," she said stiffly.

"The governor's efficient events planner," he finished. "Tom was very complimentary about you at breakfast."

She gasped, horrified that her two identities had merged to the point her impossible client had discussed her over breakfast with her lover.

"Nice to meet the real you." Steve held out his hand again, this time to shake hers. "I'd like to see you again. Tonight even. If you're free."

She blushed and shook her head. "Like I told you last night, I don't date."

"Fine. More nights like last night won't be a hardship for me."

"Look, I don't pick guys up either...or have hot one-night stands."

"Then that means I was special, which means I definitely would like a repeat of last night. If we do it twice, I'll sock anybody who dares say we ever had a one-night stand."

"I don't sleep around."

"Hey, all I'm saying is I'd like to see you again."

"No. We have to work together. Since I'm planning this event for Ryan, we'll have to have a business relationship. I'd appreciate it if you'd cool it and never speak to me about last night again. And please, please don't brag to Tom."

"What? You think I'd tell any man about you and me?"

"You could ruin my reputation."

"The last thing I want is to hurt you, Amy."

"Then stay out of my life."

"But we're planning an important event together."

"If I screw up, I'll lose my job."

"If I screw up, I'll hurt a man who's been like a second father to me. What do you say we schedule a meeting to discuss the awards banquet?"

"I'll check my calendar at the office and have my assistant, Nita, call you. We can work through her." She made her voice cold.

"I want a meeting tonight. Dinner. With you. Not Nita. I'll bet you have your calendar in that thick briefcase somewhere."

"No," she lied.

"If you don't say yes, I'll tell Tom that's the only free time I have. He'll order you to see me."

"I won't sleep with you again."

"Then you're a helluva lot better at resisting temptation than I am, darlin'."

"Don't be a jerk."

"I would have left you alone, if you hadn't shown up today and tempted me."

"Please…"

When he moved closer, a wild, pagan song drummed through her pulse. "I like you. You could like me back without half trying."

His possessive gaze raked her body and caused a wild thrill to trace through her nerves. "But I'm not going to," she whispered unsteadily.

"Why? What are you running from?"

"Nothing. I just want to be left alone."

"Then why did you make love to me last night like you would die if you didn't?"

"It was just sex."

"We both wish," he growled.

She felt a wistful little smile flicker across her lips as she remembered his body plunging inside hers. "Good sex," she conceded. She hugged herself. So good that she was so sore, she remembered she'd been in his arms every time she took the smallest step.

"Why do you hate yourself, Amy?"

"Shut up. Just shut up."

"That damn tattoo! Did that bastard whose name starts with *L* do something to you? Who the hell is he, anyway?"

She felt the blood drain from her face and the air rush from her lungs. Despite the heat, suddenly she was shivering.

"If he hurt you, if he's the reason you're so afraid, I'll hunt him down for you! I'll… I'll cut off his—"

His nearness caused her blood to roar in her ears. In another moment she'd fling herself into his arms.

"I'm not afraid because of any guy, okay?" she whispered. "Do yourself a favor and forget me. I'm not worth all this."

"You are to me."

"I could hurt you—terribly."

"I'm willing to take the risk. You want my arms around you right now, don't you? In this hellaciously hot loft? You want to feel alive, desired, loved the same as I do."

Even before he took her hand and brought it to his lips, she was melting. He looked down at her and his eyes burned her like lasers. He was so damned handsome.

He could seduce her so easily, she knew. Just holding her hand and staring at her brought her to a level of arousal she'd only known last night.

As if touching fire, she yanked her hand free and scuttled quickly away from him, groping for the ladder.

Breathing hard and blinking against tears, she gulped out, "Pigs don't sweat!"

The spell that had gripped him was broken.

"What?"

"You're a rancher. Don't you know anything? Pigs like to wallow in cool mud because they don't have sweat glands." She began climbing down the rungs.

"Hey—"

She flung herself onto the concrete floor and ran toward the barn doors.

Seven

Amy had said she wasn't afraid, but her face had gone as white as chalk, and her huge eyes had blazed with panic before she'd run. She'd looked just like his brother Jack used to look if someone so much as dared mention a car wreck.

What had gone so terribly wrong in Amy's life? Whatever it was, she couldn't handle it any better than Jack had been able to handle Ann's death after the head-on collision that had left Ann dead and him alive. His brother would still be shutting people out, just the way Amy was shutting him out now, if he hadn't fallen in love with Gloria. Steve had tried to help Jack, but Jack had rebuffed him. Madison had rejected him, too.

Steve knew better than to try to help. Still, he couldn't stop himself from tearing after Amy in a mad rush. She was almost to the barn doors when he caught her by the wrist and yanked her against his body.

"Why do you hate yourself, Amy? Why would you want to punish yourself?"

She blanched. "It's none of your business."

"You're wrong," he rasped. Bringing his arm around her, he hauled her against the solid wall of his chest. "I care about you. Doesn't that make it my business?"

She lifted her sad, shimmering gaze to his. Her lips were trembling so violently he sucked in a breath. But when she put her fists on his chest and pushed him away, he released her.

"And you care about me," he insisted.

She gulped in a breath.

"Amy, I'm going to find out. There are ways—"

"Don't you dare try. Look, I…I don't care about you. You've known me what—all of one night?"

"The best night of my life, darlin'."

"I didn't invite you into my life."

"Yes, you did. You stared at me with those big, sad eyes."

"So? I wanted to sleep with you. I admit it. Big deal. Now I want to be left alone. I'm sorry if you want more. I don't. You'll just have to accept that."

His jaw tightened.

"Just because you slept with me doesn't give you the right to push me around. Who do you think you are— threatening to find out stuff about me behind my back? The guy I fell for last night wouldn't do that. You're worse, way worse than my mother."

It was his turn to turn white and go cold. Somehow he knew that was the worst thing she could have said.

"You're right. The last thing I want is to bully you." He forced himself to take a deep breath. It was very difficult for him to turn his back on someone he loved when she was in trouble. "All right," he muttered. "Have it your way. Be miserable. Make me miserable, too."

When she turned, he followed her out of the barn into the brilliant sunshine.

"There you two are," Tom barked, waving Amy over to meet Ryan and Lily, who were standing on the front porch. No sooner had they joined the group than a late-model red Cadillac whirled past them, only to stop amidst plumes of dust in the purple shade of the big live oak in front of the ranch house.

When the couple left the motor running and stayed inside the big car, Tom introduced Amy to Ryan and Lily.

After a brief exchange, Tom's cell phone rang. Within seconds he signaled his pilot.

"Gotta go," he said to Ryan. "Got a meeting in San Antonio. Just wanted to stop by and see how things are going. Steve, it looks like you need to light a fire under that contractor of yours. Burke, I'll call you later. I've got a lot of ideas."

When Tom dashed to the helicopter, everybody stayed on the porch so they would be out of the way of flying dust when Tom's helicopter took off.

Rotors whirled and for a few seconds the helicopter hovered, causing a miniature dust storm of its own. Then Tom was above the blowing debris, waving down at them from the blue sky.

"Nice of him to stop by," Ryan said at the exact moment his cell phone rang. "Hell, it's the Red Rock PD." He snapped the phone open and held it against his ear. Even before the dust settled, Ryan's expression darkened.

Curious, but not wanting to pry, Steve stared at the Cadillac and wondered why the couple didn't get out.

"Tom's very anxious that the awards banquet be a success," Amy said to Lily, her eye on the Cadillac, as well. "He's impressed with all Ryan has done, and, frankly, so am I." She hesitated. "I'd like to talk to you both about all your various interests, your children, your careers, but especially your charity work. The governor wants this to be your party, so it needs to reflect your personality and what you've done for Texas. Tom told me, 'Ryan's the kind of Texan who makes Texas look even bigger on the map.'"

"That's so sweet of him," Lily said.

"Maybe we can talk a little today, and I'll give you my card in case you think of anything else."

"I'll give you mine, too. Call us anytime," Lily said.

She and Amy were digging in their purses for their cards as Ryan hung up. When he stared past them at the Cadillac with a glazed expression, Lily touched her husband's shoulder. "Who was that on the phone, dear? You look worried."

Ryan took a deep breath. "Gabe."

"Thunderhawk? That awful, arrogant cop who gave me that ridiculously expensive ticket?"

"You were speeding, Lily." Although his voice was gentle, Ryan didn't smile at her as he usually did. "This is about a drowning at Lake Mondo."

Amy's hand flew to her throat. Then she went still.

"For some reason Gabe thinks I can identify a body that washed up on the shore," Ryan finished.

Amy made a small choking sound. "Lake Mondo?"

"Are you okay?" Steve whispered under his breath to Amy.

Amy, who was as white as paper, looked straight ahead as she backed blindly away from the group.

"But why you, Ryan?" Lily asked. "Who does he think it is?"

"He says it's a relative of mine."

"But—"

"He suspects murder. The body was in the water several days."

Amy was still frozen. The last bit of light had gone out of her eyes.

The doors of the Cadillac slammed open. Steve, who was worried about both Amy and Ryan, frowned when a tall, dark man about his own age erupted out of the driver's side and dashed around the front of the car. Ignoring him, a voluptuous blonde in a cowgirl costume oozed out of the passenger side. Shooting Steve and Ryan a slow, high-voltage smile, she ripped her red-checkered western shirt out of the waistband of her skintight jeans and began retucking it.

Spandex, Steve thought. He should know. When the woman kept smiling at him, Steve couldn't help smiling back, even though his primary concern was for Amy, who still looked pale and frozen.

Every other man was watching the newcomer, who was still bending and twisting, pretending she was fiddling with her shirttail when in reality she was showing off her breasts and hips.

In her hokey cowgirl costume the blonde had the security guys' tongues hanging out.

Jewels sparkled when she fluffed her bleached blond hair. Steve would bet the diamonds were fakes. Same as her boobs. The red little-girl bow in her big Texas hair added a bizarre touch.

"Who's that?" Amy muttered, taking an interest in the new arrival at last when Ryan dashed down the steps to welcome them.

"Hell if I know," Steve said.

"Her jeans are so tight, you could strike a match on her hips."

Steve grinned. "Jealous?"

The skin beneath Amy's blue eyes was suddenly drawn and pale again. She looked so fragile, he wished he hadn't teased her.

"Of course not." She smoothed her hair out of her eyes and smiled at Lily. "Maybe the two of us could talk now, Lily."

"Now would be a great time."

Amy pulled out a notepad.

Steve excused himself. "If you two are going to get down to business, I think I'd better introduce myself to my guests."

When Amy and Lily nodded, Steve loped down the drive and thrust out his hand to the blonde. Her hand was soft, and she held on to his much longer than was necessary.

"Hi," she cooed. "I'm Melissa Wilkes."

"Steve Fortune."

"I know." She drew him closer and whispered, "Too bad my husband's with me, sugar."

"Introduce me, why don't you?" Steve said.

She gave a practiced sigh of regret. "Hey, Jason, baby."

Jason's dark head whipped around. Patting Ryan's shoulder, he strode over to them. "Steve Fortune?"

Steve shook his hand.

"Jason Wilkes." Jason's smile was quick and eager, his grip sure and almost too forceful. "Logan and Ryan have told me all about you and the Loma Vista." Jason's brown eyes swept the improved pastures, the native-limestone mansion and cottages, the barns, stables, cookhouse and the livestock. "Said good things. Only good things. I can see why."

Logan Fortune, Ryan's nephew, was the current CEO of Fortune TX, Ltd., Ryan's company. Although Ryan still went in most days, he served as an advisor only.

"Logan said you put all this together in the past ten years," Jason said to Steve.

"You a rancher?"

"Hope to be." Jason's eyes gleamed.

"He's a lot like you," Ryan said proudly. "You two have the same energy and ambition I had when I was your age."

"That means a lot, coming from you," Jason replied.

"If people were stock, I'd bet on you two," Ryan said. "Jason got my attention when Logan told me about a complicated oil deal Jason literally made happen."

Jason beamed as Ryan bragged about him. His smile brightened when Ryan began to talk about the old days when he'd been building his empire. Wilkes was a good listener. He said all the right things and asked the correct questions whenever there was an appropriate lull.

His dark hair was perfectly cut, his nails buffed, and his khakis and brand-name T-shirt neatly pressed. He was every bit as slick and polished as Larry Cabot and his rich, spoiled bunch had been.

Old money? Maybe. Then Steve considered Melissa. Then again maybe not. Still, guys like Wilkes used to intimidate the hell out of Steve when he'd been a kid at Yale, running around with Cabot and his fast, popular clique.

While Ryan expanded on his exploits and Jason listened, rapt, Melissa yawned and shifted her weight from one booted foot to the other until Jason frowned at her.

Steve smiled as he listened to Ryan's favorite story about his first wildcat oil well, then he noticed Lily standing alone sipping ice water under the skimpy shade of a mesquite tree. Where was Amy?

Lily's brow puckered as she watched Ryan, but Steve didn't dwell on her obvious wifely concern. Amy was gone.

Where the hell was she?

His gaze wandered from his ranch house to the barn and to the pastures. He couldn't forget how lost and sick she'd looked when Ryan had mentioned that body washing up.

He had to find her.

Amy leaned against a yellow bulldozer by the clearing where the party tents would be set up, her pencil poised where she'd been jotting notes on her legal pad so feverishly she'd broken the lead of her mechanical pencil six times. She knew because she'd counted.

Heck, she was an events planner. She was used to counting tables, chairs, centerpieces, tablecloths, silverware and on and on. Counting was in her blood.

But counting wasn't the issue. She'd broken the lead six times because ghosts were wailing in her head.

She was under dark water, her lungs exploding as she kicked her way to the surface. After gulping air, she began screaming for Lexie. When she was nearly exhausted from treading water and fighting for every breath, she drifted into her overturned boat and managed to cling to the bow line. Hours later when two fishermen motored up, she was so hysterical all she could say was, "You've got to find Lexie."

Then she was in their boat, her white-knuckled hands clutching their fiberglass boat railing. Other boats joined them, and she heard other voices yelling into the darkness while she strained to find Lexie in those black waters.

They'd motored on Lake Mondo all night long that first night and then all the next day and into the night.

When Lexie's body had washed to shore three weeks later, Lexie's father had come by Amy's parents' house and demanded to talk to the girl who'd killed his daughter. Her mother had barred the door with her own body like a protective mother bear, refusing to let him in.

"But I want to see him," Amy had said, stepping past her mother's thin, black-clad figure onto the porch.

Robert Vale had looked haggard and old. His cheekbones had stuck out through his gray, translucent skin.

His eyes had been dead and soulless, like glass marbles in a skull's eye sockets. His hair had turned white and blew about his colorless face like tufts of straw. His hands had shaken so badly he'd plunged them into his pockets.

"This is all your fault," he'd said, his tone so low and thready and yet deadly, she'd had to lean closer to hear him.

"You were driving the boat," he'd accused.

"We hit a log."

"You were going too fast or she wouldn't have been thrown out of the boat. You were wearing the only life vest. Why was that?"

"I don't know. I don't know."

"You don't deserve to live. Remember that! Not if *my* daughter's dead!"

His words had hammered into her the truth she'd lived with for eight years. They had deadened her heart and made her numb. Yet here she was—alive still. Achingly, painfully alive.

The warm June wind blowing across her face brought Amy back to the bittersweet present. As she pushed more lead out of her pencil, she couldn't resist lifting her face to the gentle breezes that rustled the grasses and made the yellow legal pages flutter.

She set her tablet on the ground. The sweet smells of grass and hay and other woodsy scents were irresistible. She wrinkled her nose, inhaling yesterday, inhaling all the yesterdays of her childhood before she and Lexie had hit their troubled adolescence and rebelled.

When Amy had been a kid, early summer used to be

her favorite time of the year. She'd made dates with Lexie to play and to ride. Summers had meant she'd been free to spend more time at Lexie's ranch. Her father had driven her out to the Vale ranch, which had seemed like paradise.

Funny, how standing here on Steve's ranch made the present blend with the past, made the poignant losses not hurt quite so much as she remembered how once the start of summer had promised endless possibilities.

Thoughts of Steve made her heart beat faster. Sometimes when he looked at her, she felt reassured instead of afraid of who she was or wasn't. He wanted to help her, to save her even. For the first time in a long time, she found herself longing for those endless possibilities that had been lost to her for so long. For the first time she wondered if happiness was possible for someone like her. She'd loved being with him.

Spending time with him again seemed as precious a goal as spending time riding and playing with Lexie had once been.

She wanted her life back. She wanted paradise again. She wanted to love and to be loved and to make those who loved her proud of her.

Love had been such an easy thing when she'd been a child. All she'd had to do was smile or put on a pretty new dress to make her father laugh and clap. Even when she was bad he'd laughed.

Oh, God, how she'd loved her parents.

The one thing she'd never wanted to do was hurt them.

The Vales had sued her parents because of the boating accident. Many of her parents' best friends had dropped them after the unflattering newspaper articles about her. Her mother, who wanted prestige more than anything, had been so devastated she'd been hospitalized for depression. For long months she'd been too lethargic to work. Her law practice had suffered.

Amy never again wanted to hurt them or anybody else she loved.

And that meant she had to keep saying no to Steve. Because she could love him.

Don't think about Steve.

Just be.

That's good enough for now.

A dirt lane led toward the brush that edged the clearing near the bulldozer. The lane continued through the brush, she supposed.

Where exactly did it go?

Setting her briefcase on the ground, she pulled the pins and rubber band out of her hair, so that it could blow freely in the warm, summer wind. Then she headed down the little trail toward the tangle of juniper, mesquite and persimmons that wound through the brush.

Like a curious child, she followed the path until she came to a grassy clearing beneath the trees and saw a pool in this heart of darkness, its brown surface as smooth and gleaming as polished glass. Beside the pool was a concrete bench. She went to it and, placing her hands on her upper thighs, she sat down slowly.

When she bent over, she saw her reflection in the pool's luminous depths. With the dark trees all around and her bright hair cascading in ripples of gold on either side of her slim face, she looked like wood nymph, like a girl without a care in the world. The water washed all her sins away.

Clasping her hands in her lap, she shut her eyes and breathed in the sweetness of the air.

Usually she hated to be still for a moment for fear the demons would attack. But this was different somehow.

No longer aware of herself so much, she listened to the birds and the rustlings of the leaves and the little scratching sounds squirrels made as they scuttled across the ground.

She didn't know how long she sat there, but it was darker and cooler when she opened her eyes again. A silver fish jumped, casting sparkling rivulets into the water. She felt a strange peace. The light and shadow shimmering above her and upon the pool's surface seemed magical.

She loved it out here.

She hadn't loved any place so much in years.

She understood why Steve had fought so hard to build this place, just as she knew she would want to come here again and again.

Not that she could.

Behind her she heard the sharp crackle of leaves. A large animal, she thought, following the same trail she had. A thirsty cow maybe.

Slightly nervous, she twisted around and waited for whatever or whoever it was. Within seconds she found herself gazing through veils of shadows and sparkling light at a black mare and a tall, dark, broad-shouldered man following behind her. Noche walked with a noticeable limp.

Amy got up slowly and went to them.

Steve smiled at her but did not speak, at least not in words. Again, for a timeless moment, she felt that uncanny connection to this man she hardly knew. Then Noche came up and nuzzled her hand with her warm nose.

"Are you okay?" Steve murmured.

"I wish I had a carrot to give her," Amy said.

"Tomorrow. We'll bring a whole bag of carrots with us."

He sounded so sure they had tomorrow.

"I love it here," she said.

"You belong here."

She looked up at him. "For the first time in a long time I feel what I'm really feeling. I don't know what's happening to me. It's so strange."

"You're supposed to feel what you feel, rather than pretend or ignore your feelings. That's the only way Noche knows how to be."

"She's a horse."

"Which means she's a lot smarter than most people."

"True," Amy agreed.

At the sound of her name, Noche had looked up from nibbling grasses near their feet, the wisdom of the ages in her gentle gaze.

"If you get quiet long enough, you figure things out," he said. "Ranchers are lucky. We work the land. We know its rhythms. Rain, drought. Winter, summer. Birth, death."

Death. Amy shivered.

"It's an ancient way of life that teaches ancient truths."

"I used to spend a lot of summer days on a ranch like

this. Now I stay so busy planning all sorts of events that I can't hear myself think. I live on the phone."

"We chase success until the chase kills us. We're taught that making money is all that matters."

"That's what my mother believes."

"My father's had a hard time accepting that I'd rather ranch than get really rich."

"I used to ride," Amy said. "I loved it so much." She sighed. "I...I haven't ridden in years."

"Well, then, you're like Noche. She used to be ridden."

"What happened?"

"She was injured."

"What's wrong with her?"

"She has a problem with her stifle."

Amy knew the stifle was comparable to the knee in humans.

"She's got a cyst," Steve said. "There's an operation, but it's so tricky and risky to the other stifle that, in my opinion, it might as well be inoperable. I just haven't got the guts to put her through the operation. My vet told me he'd put her down for me."

Amy's heart caught at the sadness in his deep voice. Why did terrible things like this have to happen? Even to horses? She started to touch Steve's arm and barely managed to stop herself from doing so.

"Oh, no. How old is she?"

"Three years."

"That's too bad."

"Yes. Well, I'm not putting her down."

"So she's your thousand-pound pet."

"I guess some people would see it that way. Others

like my father would say she's a lousy investment." His dark gaze followed Noche. "But I think she's beautiful." His drawl had thickened.

Steve was staring at Amy with an intensity that made her breath race in confusion. His eyes were midnight-black, his pupils indistinguishable from the irises. What was she going to do about her growing attraction for this incredible man?

"Noche loves me without question. She is a beautiful, intelligent animal." His low, caressing tone was as soft as a lover's. "Perfect or not, I need her."

A lump formed in her throat. "That seems like a strange thing for a rancher to say," she whispered, wondering why her voice caught.

"It's the truth."

The conviction in his husky baritone and his brilliant, dark eyes made her want things she had no right to want.

"I...I don't know what to say."

"Say you'll go to dinner with me tonight."

Her heart leaped. "To plan the governor's awards banquet?"

"If you need an excuse like that, fine." His voice had a raw edge now. "I want to get to know you better. No sex, I swear. Just conversation." He grinned. "As long as you don't wear spandex." His deep voice had gone softer. "Or something low enough that shows off your tattoo, which is sexier than hell, by the way."

Her hands shook a little, and she began to perspire. Placing her hand against her throat for fear he'd see how rapid her pulse was, she struggled to keep her voice calm.

Just say no, she thought.

"I suppose we do have a lot to talk about," she murmured a little hesitantly. "But not tonight. I have a seminar to conduct in Houston tomorrow afternoon and I need to get ready. I may be up all night downloading the presenters' speeches into laptops for the attendees. I could make it tomorrow night, though."

His quick grin was so hot it scorched her bones. "Did you say yes because I won't put Noche down?"

She ignored his question. "We do have a lot to talk about," she said primly. "Lists to make for the awards banquet."

"I can't wait," he muttered. His grin widened. "Making lists is my favorite thing." His teasing eyes were deep and dark again as he gazed at her. Not trusting herself, she turned to stare at his beautiful black horse.

Why was it that the more she was with him, the more she wanted to be with him? The more she *had* to be with him?

"Tomorrow night I'll have to drive straight from the airport to whatever restaurant you choose," she said.

"Why don't you meet me at the Shiny Pony? Around seven? That way if your plane's late, I'll have plenty to do while I wait."

She had a date, sort of. She wouldn't have to work late to avoid the loneliness and fear she sometimes felt when four empty walls of her apartment closed in around her.

She felt like throwing her arms around him, like jumping up and down. Afraid that if she smiled he'd see how eager she was, she bit her lips and looked away.

He grinned again. "I can't believe you said yes."

"It's just a planning session," she said, avoiding his gaze.

Eight

Steve felt as nervous as a teenager on his first date as he drove toward Austin. It was six-thirty. He'd be late to meet Amy, judging from the looks of the thickening traffic on I-35 on the north side of San Marcos.

Tonight he had to go slow with Amy. She was fragile. Despite the hot sex, he didn't really know her. Just thinking about her made him so anxious to see her, he wanted to stomp on the accelerator.

To distract himself, he inserted a tape about Greek mythology. The narrator had barely begun to describe Achilles sulking in his tent when Steve yanked the tape out and flung it onto the passenger's seat.

The Greeks were too deep for him tonight. He picked up his cell phone and punched in Ryan's number, intending to apologize for not calling sooner.

"Have you read the paper?" Ryan demanded without preliminaries.

"No. Why?"

"Thunderhawk's accusing me of murder! And he's leaked it to the media! Every paper in central Texas is running front-page stories about it. It's all over the Internet, too."

"Murder?"

"Three little bullet holes in the skull need to be accounted for."

"Hell."

"The medical examiner says the deceased is in his early thirties. The poor bastard washed up with a lot of his face eaten away by aquatic creatures. He had no identification—other than the blasted Fortune crown birthmark. There it was—like an ugly brand right above his bloated, decomposing right buttock!"

"I should've gone with you."

"When I said I'd never seen him before in my life, Thunderhawk demanded that I account for every hour of my time this past week! And when I couldn't—"

Steve's temple was throbbing painfully. "Hold on."

A thousand red brake lights were flashing ahead of him. He hit his own brakes hard.

Ryan continued. "The arrogant bastard said he'd get the truth out of me one way or the other. I think he tipped off the papers in order to put additional pressure on me."

Steve remembered the stark pain in Amy's eyes yesterday. He'd wanted to be in an upbeat, positive mood for her, but now this. Selfishly he almost wished he hadn't called Ryan. How could he give her the attention she needed when he was worried sick about his mentor and relative?

"Just a second!" Steve felt his mouth crimp in a taut line even before the brake lights of the eighteen-wheeler directly in front of his truck flared red. Steve slammed on his own brakes so fast, he hurtled forward, causing his seat belt to lock.

"Surely Thunderhawk is just fishing," Steve muttered as he squinted at his rearview mirror to make sure the eighteen-wheeler behind him didn't ram him. Not that he could do anything to prevent a wreck. He was a sitting duck. Rush hour traffic had him boxed in on all sides. He was in a hurry, and he wasn't going anywhere fast. How long would Amy wait on him at his bar? He needed to call Jeff and tell him to stall her. No way could he get off the phone until Ryan was done venting.

"Thunderhawk won't let up. He's asking questions, but he acts like he already knows all the answers. He's got everybody in the police department suspecting me. Everybody in Red Rock, too. Hell, everybody in Texas by now."

"It can't be that bad."

"The lead article today in the Austin newspaper makes it sound like I'm the shooter. You know how self-righteous all the busybodies in Red Rock are. People I've known all my life barely spoke to me or so much as glanced my way when I bought a couple of hunting knives in the hardware store this morning. They treated me like dirt!"

"Good thing I haven't read the paper yet."

Ryan didn't laugh.

When Steve's truck crawled to the top of a hill, he saw that the traffic was stalled for miles. *Damn.* Amy would be gone by the time he got to Austin.

Why hadn't he left the ranch earlier for his dinner date? He wished to hell he could say or do something that would make Ryan feel better, too. Hell, what he really wanted was to hang up and call Jeff.

"So, why the hell does Thunderhawk suspect you?"

"I wish I knew." Ryan's bitter voice trailed off. "I kept telling them I never saw the dead guy before. I've said that so many times I'm sick of saying it."

"You really don't have the slightest idea who he might be? Any missing relatives?"

"N-no."

When Steve caught the hesitation in his mentor's voice, his gut clenched.

"I finally told Thunderhawk I won't answer any more of his questions without my lawyer present."

"Why?"

"Because the criminal justice system in this country sucks. Because there's a couple of days and nights when I was home alone…and Lily was in San Antonio."

Again Steve caught that hesitant note in Ryan's low voice.

"Did you talk to anybody on the phone those nights? Lily?"

"N-no."

"But you always—"

"Damnation! Now you're accusing me!"

The phone went dead.

Steve stared at his phone in disbelief. What was going on? Had Ryan hung up on him? Was he lying? Lily and he always called each other when they were apart. Was he hiding something?

Steve gave Ryan five minutes to cool off before he dialed him back, only to get his voice mail.

Steve apologized curtly and hung up.

Ryan had Caller ID. Was he gone, or was he just avoiding him? And why had he gotten so angry?

If Steve didn't know better, he would have thought Ryan was acting guilty as hell.

Steve still had Ryan on his mind when he raced into the Shiny Pony half an hour late. Then he saw Amy in a tight, low-cut halter top and skirt perched on a bar stool.

Wow!

Even from across the room, she looked so golden and gorgeous, he could get hot from just looking at those long legs of hers, not to mention her face and body. Close up, she stunned him.

Her eyes lit up the instant she saw him. Her shy, radiant smile was open and sweet and flooded him with joy. She lured him like a siren, yet she had the kind of girl-next-door looks that would have fooled his mother.

She was sexier than hell. Maybe it was the halter top that fitted her like a glove, causing even her small breasts to spill over the top. She'd slung a demure long-sleeved jacket across her lap. She'd probably worn the jacket all day. He damn sure hoped so.

"Sorry I'm late," he said. "Traffic."

"My plane was late, too. Still, I…I'm glad you got here when you did. Two guys asked me to dance. Jeff had to talk to them."

Not for the first time Steve was glad he'd hired Jeff. "Want a drink? How about a Flirtita?"

"Maybe just some white wine at the restaurant. I was up all night working. If I drink now, I might fall asleep. What restaurant did you decide on?"

"Chez Marie is right around the corner. Ever been there?"

"N-not for a long time."

Her words hung suspended for a crystalline moment, and he caught the doubt in her low tone. The haunted look was back in her eyes.

"If you'd prefer somewhere else…"

"No."

He sensed that somehow he'd made a poor choice. Not that she was about to tell him why.

When he sat down beside her, she hopped up so fast he wondered if she regretted agreeing to meet him.

"I'm starved," she said. "A couple of mikes went out during the presentations. I had to work through lunch."

"Okay, we can go now. But we don't have to go to Chez Marie."

"That's fine."

Then why did she sound so doubtful? Wishing she felt easier around him, he stood up, too. Hell, they'd slept together. Why were they so damn tense around each other?

Steve glanced toward the bar and saw that Jeff and

the rest of his wait staff were watching them intently, as curious as a bunch of gossipy busybodies in Red Rock.

Damn. Suddenly he was glad she was edgy. The faster they got the hell out of here, the better.

The early evening heat felt heavy as they walked over to Chez Marie. Not that Amy seemed to notice. For a woman who'd had a long night and a hard day, she damn sure walked fast. Soon she'd sprinted ahead of him. Not that that was all bad. Her skirt was so tight, he got a thrill from watching her hips wiggle. And he wasn't the only guy on the block who admired her.

He was glad when they made it inside the cool, dark restaurant. But no sooner had he started relaxing, because he wasn't going to have to slug some jerk over her, than her shy eyes grew big and started darting everywhere.

"Looking for somebody? Old boyfriend, darlin'?"

Some jerk whose name starts with the damn letter *L* maybe?

She whirled, her eyes so dark and huge with misery, he regretted his question. She started to defend herself, but she merely shrugged and avoided his gaze. Long minutes ticked by as they stood in the doorway, neither knowing what to say to the other.

Finally a young, sunburned waiter rushed up to them. He grinned at Amy a little too boldly, and she smiled too brightly as well.

"Good evening. I'm Liam," he said. "Reservations?"

"Two for Fortune," Steve answered.

Liam picked up some menus and led them to their table.

Liam. There was a name that started with an *L*. Steve was wondering if that was a bad omen when Amy took his arm and clung. Her touch lightened his mood considerably.

"This is my mother's favorite restaurant," Amy whispered in a low, conspiratorial voice on the way to their table.

At last a clue. "I picked it to impress you, not to upset you. You know, it's not too late to go somewhere else. I want you to be able to relax."

"This is great."

Then they were at their table, which was in a shadowy, secluded corner exactly as Steve had requested. When Liam pulled Amy's chair out and handed her her napkin, she sat down and took her time daintily unfolding it while Steve ordered a bottle of wine.

Steve liked watching her long, slim fingers smooth the napkin even though she seemed to fuss with it too much.

"Amy, are you okay?"

She let the napkin be, looked up and scanned the room again before daring to meet his eyes.

"We can still leave," he said.

She went still. Then she leaned back in her chair and gulped in a big breath. "M-maybe it's time I started facing a few of my demons."

Not the kind of date I had in mind, but hell, just being out with her again was a start.

"Meaning your parents?" he said.

"Just my mother." She chewed her bottom lip and looked away.

"I'd love to meet both of them."

"And they'd love to meet you. Especially Mother. Believe me, she wants to know every single detail of my life. She would love you."

As he watched Amy's fingers twisting her napkin again, he felt sure that wasn't a point in his favor.

"She's a successful, high-profile trial attorney, right?"

"Yes. Fortunately, she works nearly all the time. If she didn't, she'd drive us both crazy. Her excuse for being so bossy and critical is that she has high expectations for me."

Steve knew the type.

Mindful of the fragile stemware glittering on their table, he reached across the white tablecloth and took her hand.

"Facing demons wasn't exactly what I hoped we'd be doing together tonight," he said. "I wanted us to have fun."

"But you said no sex."

He caught his breath. Just her saying the *S* word made the air between them sizzle. He couldn't believe when she smiled at him before looking shyly away.

"What I really want is to get to know you…and to be your friend. That could be fun, too."

She laughed nervously. "If I let the demons loose while you're here, maybe you can battle them for me."

He squeezed her hand. "I'd be glad to."

He shouldn't have said that, but it was hard for him to not help someone he cared about.

When he let her hand go, she picked at her thumbnail. Then she opened her menu and they discussed the night's specials. When Liam returned to take their orders, they both chose salmon and a salad.

In the long, awkward silence that followed, Steve finally began to talk because someone had to. She leaned forward eagerly. At first her face seemed too pale and strained in the flickering candlelight. Every time the door behind him opened, her eyes shot to it, widening with alarm.

Finally he shut up. "I know you had a long day with lots of people. You're probably sick and tired of talking."

"No, please. I love listening to you."

When he began anew, she sat ramrod straight, still saying nothing. At least after a few sips of her Chardonnay, she quit looking at the door every time it opened.

He told a joke, and although she didn't laugh, she smiled a little.

Inspired, he embellished the events of his day—the good parts, before Ryan had upset him with the news about the body. When she still didn't offer to say anything, Steve forced himself to think up more small talk.

Steve discussed the heat, of course, always a favorite topic in Texas during the summer. He went off on an idiotic tangent about how the asphalt was so hot the warm air smelled of tar and seemed as thick and sticky. He stopped himself again.

Give her a chance to talk, too, you fool.

"I love that smell, too," she finally whispered.

Then she looked away, and he saw that her eyes were sad again. Was she remembering her ghost?

When she still didn't say more, he began to tell her about his ranch. To his surprise, her face lit up.

"I spent most of the morning and the afternoon out in the pastures at Loma Vista, which, by the way, is my favorite way to spend a day."

"I loved it out there."

"My foreman says we've had so much rain the past two years, it looks like we're going to have a bumper calf crop this fall."

"Really?"

"A lot of my calves are going to weigh at least seven hundred pounds by August."

"And that's good?"

"Yeah. Really good. Off-the-charts good."

Liam brought their salads. Steve waited until she lifted her fork before he did the same.

She leaned close enough so that he caught the fragrance of violets. Her golden head was cocked at a cute angle, and her eyes shone with excitement as she swirled the golden liquid in her wineglass. She seemed to hang on his every word, as if what he did mattered to her. Suddenly he felt prouder of all that he'd accomplished on his ranch than he'd ever felt before and was bursting to tell her more.

But not now. He had to get her talking. How else was he ever going to get to know her?

"So, how was your day?" he prompted.

She stabbed at a piece of goat cheese. "Okay, I guess. Busy. Did your construction people show up?" she replied, deftly sidetracking him.

"Around ten. Sometimes I wonder if they'll ever get the house and barns and outbuildings done in time for the banquet."

"If you don't keep on them, they won't. Oh boy, how I hate deadlines," she said. "I could tell you horror stories."

"I'd like to hear one."

"There's a lot of pressure these days to plan events without much lead time. If you can meet commitments ahead of schedule, then you have more time to deal with whatever goes wrong."

"Do things always go wrong?"

"Do they ever!" She laughed. "That's why I get paid. I put out all the brush fires. Take the presenters last night. One of them didn't e-mail me his presentation until two in the morning, so I couldn't download it until he did. And then those mikes today. I make decisions, solve those last-minute problems. I stay up all night if necessary. The secret is not to sweat the small stuff. When something goes wrong, you just have to fix it and go on."

Her brows crinkled, and she set her fork down and stared past him.

"How come you look so puzzled all of a sudden?" he murmured.

"I just realized that if I applied that to my life, I'd—"

Liam's arrival with the rest of their meal interrupted her. Steve wasn't done with his salad, but he shoved it to one side and attacked his fish as soon as she lifted her fork.

"The salmon is good, really good," he said after he took his first bite.

"So good it literally melts in your mouth," she agreed, tasting hers. "I love this rich honey glaze they drizzled all over it. I've used these people to cater lots of events."

After that, they ate in silence for a while. He couldn't help noticing that all the other couples around them spoke to each other more eagerly than they concentrated on their meal. He put his fork down and looked at her, wishing she'd say something, anything.

She put her fork down and swallowed a deep breath. "I'm sorry I'm such poor company."

"But you're not."

"Like I told you, I'm out of practice when it comes to…dating."

His throat tightened when he realized she saw tonight as a date, too.

"That's fine. Even though we started off with a bang, we can go slowly…as slowly as you need us to."

"I…I come with a lot of baggage."

He thought about Ryan and Lily and their complicated pasts. He also remembered standing at the altar alone while "Here Comes the Bride" played endlessly and no bride came down the aisle. Who didn't come with baggage?

"Got any drowned corpses in your closets with birthmarks on them?" he teased.

As soon as she lifted her head, he saw the grief flooding her eyes. His stomach knotted. He pushed his salmon aside.

"Sorry. I had this really weird conversation with Ryan earlier. I wasn't going to mention it, but I guess I can't get it off my mind."

"It's all right," she said softly. "How could you know what to say or not say? I haven't given you many clues." She hesitated.

"About yesterday…" She swallowed, looking anxiously at the door again. "I…I got upset because of that drowning in Lake Mondo."

"I noticed. I wondered why you ran off." He stopped, wishing he could give her more than a blank stare.

Her hands began twisting the napkin in her lap into a tight melon-colored rope.

"A long time ago a friend of mine drowned in Lake Mondo."

He waited, hoping for more.

"Her name was Lexie," she said.

Had he ever heard more sadness in any voice?

"We searched for her body for days. I…I cried her name until I was hoarse."

"So, the tattooed *L* stands for Lexie?"

She nodded. "We were still kids when we got those awful tattoos. Lexie got an *A* over her heart. She did it first, you see. My mother found out and forbade me—"

"But you snuck off and did it anyway?"

"Back then Lexie and I did everything together. But Mother was right—as always. I regretted the tattoo the next day. If I'd done everything she told me, nothing would—"

She stopped. When her eyes widened with shock at something she saw behind him, he tensed. Pressing her lips together, she ducked lower, as if attempting to hide behind his broad-shouldered body.

"Why didn't you ever tell me you regretted that tattoo, dear?" came a deep, throaty voice from behind his left shoulder.

"Mother," Amy squeaked. "I didn't see you."

"Then why are you cowering behind your handsome friend?"

"Where's Daddy?" Amy said.

"Parking the Volvo. You know how I hate valet parking. Sit up straight, dear, or you'll be big in the gut way before you're my age."

Amy sat up rigidly, but her face was ashen.

"Introduce me, dear."

"Oh, of course. Sorry. This is my, er, client, Steve Fortune. Mr. Fortune is hosting the Hensley-Robinson Awards Banquet that I'm planning for Tom."

"Oh! Fortune as in *the* Fortunes?" Her mother was laughing almost giddily now. She leaned over Steve, staring at him, her sharp black eyes missing nothing.

When he held his hand out, she pumped it harder than most men would have.

She was attractive as were lots of rich women of an age, women who could afford good haircuts, makeup, clothes and plastic surgery. A smooth cap of glossy jet hair fell softly against her severe face. Tall and regally slim in a striking black suit, she had the commanding presence of a woman long used to getting her way.

"So," she murmured, "how are you related to Ryan Fortune?"

"Distantly," Steve answered succinctly.

"What's this awful news in the paper about him being involved with that drowning victim?"

Steve stiffened.

"Why, there was a terrible story in today's paper about it. Several stories, as a matter of fact. Simply everybody's talking about it." Her throaty voice held a warning, even as her shrewd eyes homed in on Amy's pale, stricken face. "Did you see the front page, dear?"

"You know I left the house at five to fly to Houston, Mother."

"Well, don't read it. Not tonight. Not until you call me."

Amy looked so crushed, Steve knew he had to get her out of here. Dark shadows under her eyes gave her that haunted look again, and her hands were shaking.

"It was great meeting you," Steve said abruptly. "Amy and I both had long days. I think we'd better call it an evening."

Her mother took the hint and said goodbye. When she'd gone, Steve leaned closer to Amy. "Are you okay?"

"Sure."

"You don't look okay."

"You said we were going."

"So, we're back to not talking again?"

"I don't want to burden—"

"Just tell me why your mother upsets you so much."

"She always takes charge."

"Only because you let her."

"I can't forget that if I'd done what she said years ago, Lexie would still be alive. I always feel so guilty when I'm around her. I've disappointed her so deeply. I'm her only daughter. She used to be so proud of me, and now I'm this huge disappointment."

"Maybe she was screaming so loudly, you couldn't hear yourself think. You can't live your life according to other people's views. Not even your parents'. You've got to listen to yourself. Maybe it's time you give up being who she wants and become yourself."

"Whoever that is. Look…I don't feel very well all of a sudden. I don't want to talk about her."

"Hell, neither do I, but she seems to be at the center of whatever's wrong in your life."

"No, she isn't! It's all my fault!"

"Do you blame yourself for Lexie's death?"

Amy lurched out of her chair and threw her tangled napkin in her plate. "I knew this couldn't work. I'm too messed up. I don't want to mess you up, too!"

"Whatever's wrong, you can fix it."

"You really think life's that easy?"

"It is if you don't give up on yourself."

"You don't know anything. You've never hurt anyone in your whole life! There are some things you can't take back!"

She stumbled toward the door. Without looking at the bill, he tossed two hundred-dollar bills on the table and raced after her. Vaguely he was aware of her parents' anguished faces. Everybody else was watching them, too.

Not that he cared, when he sprang between her and the front door.

"Let's just forget this," she said. "Forget the other night…."

When she tried to move past him, he grabbed her arm and held on tight. "No. I want us to work this out. I care about you too much, Amy."

"You're a fool, then. There is no *us*. It won't work. Like I said, I'm too messed up."

"Do you want to stay stuck in this hell you've created for yourself for the rest of your life?"

Struggling to pull her arm free, she went even whiter. But he was too far gone to care.

"Take your hands off me. You're making a scene," she whispered.

His gaze veered toward her stricken-looking father and mother, toward Liam, whose unsmiling face held vague menace now.

"I was trying to help," Steve whispered. "But all right, you win."

As abruptly as he'd seized her, he let her go. Raising both hands, he backed up and stood still as a statue until she flung the door open and ran out. Then he stormed out after her and loped alongside her the whole way to her car. When she pulled out her keys and accidentally unlocked all her doors, he sprang into the passenger side.

She was sobbing as she jammed her key into the ignition. "Get out or you'll be sorry!"

"Amy, you're too upset to drive."

A flick of her wrist had her keys jingling again. The engine growled to life. "This is all your fault. You had to pry."

"Let me drive you home."

"Last chance, buster. Get out now!"

"Amy, please—"

"I said get out!"

He slammed his door and folded his wide arms across his thick chest.

"Buckle your seat belt," she muttered as she snapped her own together.

"Amy—"

"Last chance. Get out!"

When he stayed where he was, she stomped on the accelerator and wheeled out of the parking lot so fast her tires screamed. He caught the acrid stench of burning rubber.

"For God's sake, Amy—"

"Shut up! Just shut up! Do you think I want to be unhappy forever? Is that what you think?"

At the sound of more hoarse, racking sobs, he turned. Pale brilliance sifted from a streetlight and bleached all color from her wet, tortured face.

"Aw, hell, darlin'. I've gone and made you cry."

Nine

Ignoring Steve, Amy hunched forward over the steering wheel and focused on her driving. She was frowning at the flying road. Steve took a deep, fortifying breath as the Toyota zipped frenetically through traffic, surging north up a wide lane of Congress Avenue toward the brightly lit capitol building. Steve cinched his seat belt as tightly as it would go and then gave his shoulder harness a yank as the Camry weaved around other cars chaotically.

One second she was honking at a red truck in front of her that was stopped at a light. In the next she was racing around it, running the light, causing several oncoming cars to slam on their brakes and nearly ram each other to avoid hitting her.

"Do you have a death wish?" Steve ground out through gritted teeth.

Clenching her jaw, she leaned even farther forward, not bothering to answer him.

"What about me, Amy? Do you want to kill me, too?"

She whitened.

"What about those other people out there? Kids even?"

A muscle jerked in her cheek, but she merely pressed her lips together all the more tightly.

"Amy, what's the matter with you? At least get out of town before you drive like a maniac."

She kept her head lowered, her narrowed eyes fixed on the road, her lips still clamped together. But he breathed easier as she let up on the accelerator. For a few minutes she drove at a more reasonable speed, even stopping for all the lights, only gunning it when they turned green. But no sooner did she hit Mo-Pac, the north-south freeway on the western side of Austin, than she stomped on the gas pedal again. Instantly they were flying north, lane hopping, passing streams of cars and trucks.

"Do you always rebel when your mother pulls your strings?"

"Shut up! You're pulling them, too!" She tapped the gas pedal harder.

Maybe talking to her wasn't such a good idea.

Tires squealing, she swerved off Mo-Pac onto Ranch Road 2222. A few years ago it had been a twisting rural road. Now it was a busy thoroughfare that ran through posh, hilly, northwest Austin. She zoomed up and down the steep cedar-covered hills, sped around dangerous curves so fast they skidded onto the shoulder several times. At one point when they careened over the top of a hill, they had a breath-taking view off to their left of all of West Austin, in-cluding the Colorado River and the famous red 360 Bridge.

Not that Steve was in any mood to enjoy the scen-ery. He was too worried about Amy. Her face was still ashen. Her blue eyes were wild and laser bright. She was out of control, and the Toyota was slicing through the flying dark at a hundred miles an hour.

The Camry's tires screamed as she made a turn too fast. When his shoulder harness caught, he held his breath. Artificially lit Tuscan villas and oversized Prov-ençal cottages bled past them in splashes of garish color. When she came upon a slow-moving truck too fast, she hit the brakes so hard he had to brace a hand against the dash to keep from flying forward.

She passed the truck on the right. He shot her a glance and thought better of saying anything. But when they came upon a second truck at the top of the hill and she had to hit the brakes again, that was all he could take.

"Amy!"

Glassy-eyed, she stared ahead. He wondered if she had forgotten he was there. His brother Jack had nearly died when Ann had driven out of control like this. She'd slammed head-on into a truck, killing both herself and the truck driver. It had taken a guilt-stricken Jack years to get over that accident.

Steve had had enough.

"Is this how you killed Lexie?"

She banged her fists against the steering wheel and screamed. Tears of anguish rained down her cheeks.

Instead of slowing down, she pushed the gas pedal to the floor.

He leaned over, grabbed the gearshift and downshifted into neutral. Then he yanked the keys out of the ignition.

"What are you doing?" she screamed, fighting to control the car.

"Pull over. You're in no shape to drive."

"Give me the keys!"

She was straddling the center line as they hurtled over the top of a hill. A Cadillac was in their lane, driving too slowly. In the distance he saw the lights of an oncoming car.

"Go ahead! Kill me the way you killed your best friend! Kill all those other drivers out there, too!"

Amy honked, hit the brakes and spun the wheel to the right. The Toyota fishtailed on loose gravel and flew crazily to the left across the double yellow lines into the oncoming lane. The other car honked and swerved, missing them by inches as it whizzed past.

Then they were off the road, sliding endlessly in more gravel before the car skidded into a log, stopping so abruptly Steve was thrown forward.

His forehead smacked the windshield, and everything went black.

When he came to seconds later, he was aware of violets, aware of Amy's trembling arms cradling his head as she dabbed at something oozing above his right eye.

"Wake up. Don't die. Don't die," she whispered in a subdued tone through strangled tears. "Please don't die."

"Are you okay now?" he asked.

"Me? Are *you* okay?"

"I'll live. What about you?"

Before she could reply, a fist rammed against her window. When she opened the door, a man with a black cowboy hat and a cigarette dangling out of his mouth grabbed her arm and yanked her from the car by her arm.

"What's wrong with you, girl? I've been behind you since Mo-Pac. You drunk or high on somethin'?"

"I was upset."

The man stared at her hard. Finding no sign of drunkenness, he finally released her. "Don't you know a car's the same as a lethal weapon? You could've killed somebody."

"I…I'm sorry," she said, weeping with genuine remorse as she rubbed her arm. "I shouldn't have driven like that. I… My passenger's hurt."

The stranger leaned past her and studied Steve. "You okay in there, mister?"

"I'm fine," Steve said even though he was starting to feel a little shaky. Ignoring the tremor in his hands, he opened the door and got out. "I've got the car keys." He jingled them. "I'm going to drive her home if the car's all right."

"Okay, young lady. You'd better not drive like a wild hellion again. Sooner or later your luck always runs out."

Amy swallowed convulsively.

"I was gonna call 911," the man said, "but your friend here seems responsible. Don't you ever forget, girl, cars aren't toys. Nobody has the right to drive like that—ever!" He turned to Steve. "I'll wait and make sure your car starts before I leave."

"Thanks," Steve said as he knelt and looked under the car. He walked around it before leading Amy to the passenger seat. Then he went around the back of the car and slid behind the wheel.

Even though the Toyota started, he popped the hood, got out and looked under it. When he finally backed away from the log, he got out and inspected the damage one last time.

"A few scratches on the bumper, but not many," he said as he got back inside the car. "The cut on my head is just a scratch, too. We got off lucky. Real lucky."

"This time." Amy was shaking too violently to say more.

"Where do you live?"

"Off Enfield Road."

He felt fine now, although he wasn't in the mood for conversation. Apparently, she wasn't either. She stared out her window, and he focused on the road. They drove south, back to town in tense silence. Ten minutes later when he pulled into the drive of the address she'd given him and he saw the tall, ultramodern limestone mansion and enormous, tiled pool, he whistled.

"Nice," he said, his low tone a little edgy.

"All I've got is the garage apartment. The owner's a divorcee with a teenager. Cheryl lets me live here because I'm additional security."

"Don't tell me your mother arranged this?"

"How did you know?"

He wrenched the keys from the ignition and turned and studied Amy's lovely white face that was framed by glimmering golden silky waves. Her eyes held fresh guilt along with that deep, impenetrable sadness that always tore him in two.

"Easy," he said as he got out. "She probably calls Cheryl from time to time to check up on you."

"That's right." Amy opened her door, and rock music blasted them.

He winced at the loud music, which was the last thing he needed. "Where the hell's that coming from?" he muttered.

"Kate's probably at the pool."

"Kate?" Then he got it. "Right, the teenager." He sighed. "Impossible species. They should all be exiled to another planet until they're twenty-one at least."

"She lives in the main house with her mom."

"She's a bit spoiled from the sound and look of it," he said.

"It's not her fault."

"Right. She's misunderstood by her mean old mom."

"Her mean old dad."

On their way to Amy's apartment, they had to pass the pool and the kid. Kate was curled up on a chaise longue, sipping a glass of iced tea. At least, he hoped it was tea. She had huge dark glasses, blue spiked hair and big pouty lips. Her yellow string bikini didn't cover much, so it was easy to count her piercings, of which she had way too many. Rings shot sparks at Steve from her navel, eyebrows, lips, ears and tongue as her blue head bobbed back in forth in time to the shrill beat of electronic vibrations that passed for music these days. The lyrics were streams of curses screamed at a shrill volume loud enough to puncture the eardrums of any mammal unlucky enough to be within ten blocks.

"That music's obscene," Steve said.

"She's just crying out for attention."

"Lucky girl. She's about to get it. Introduce me, why don't you?" The nerves in his eye pulsed as savagely as the beat.

"Hi, Kate," Amy yelled from her stairs. When Kate ignored her, Amy cupped her mouth with her hands and screamed, "This is my friend, Steve."

Kate yawned and turned the music slightly lower. "What happened to your friend?" She pointed to her own right eye and then made a fist as if she was about to sock herself. "He get in a fight or something?"

"Or something," Steve mumbled. "Kid, would you mind turning it down a little? Amy and I need to talk."

Her pouty lips puffed up. "Did you get so fresh, she slapped you?"

That did it. Steve strode toward the pool. "Are you going to turn that down or not?"

"This is my house, you know," Kate said sullenly. "You can't come here and order me around like I'm *your* kid or something."

God help him, if his kid ever acted like her...

"Is your mother here? I'd like to talk to her."

The kid's smirk held triumph. "She's out on a date." Kate lifted her iced-tea glass in a mock toast.

"And she left you behind? I wonder why?"

"What do you know about anything?" The girl slammed her drink down so hard it spilled everywhere.

"I know if I lived next door I'd call the cops. That's

what you want, isn't it? Then your mom would have to come home."

"What do you know about anything?"

"That's happened before," Amy interjected.

Kate's lip protruded even further.

Steve walked up to the girl. "Turn that down. *Please.*"

Kate shook her blue spiky head. "If you don't like it, go home." She twisted the knob and made it louder.

With one swift movement he grabbed the boom box and headed toward the deep end of the pool.

Kate got up and ran up to him. "Give that back!"

He dropped the boom box into the water. The music strangled after two gurgles.

"You can't do—" Kate bit her lip as he strode past her up the stairs to Amy's apartment.

He didn't look back at her as he climbed the stairs. "Sorry about that," he said to Amy once he was inside the honey-colored walls of her apartment. "I don't know why she got to me. I guess I'm not much on letting kids call the shots."

"It's my fault. I upset you, and you're hurt. There's a limit to what anybody can take. But she's not so bad. She's just a mixed-up little girl."

"Who'll grow up into a mixed-up young woman. She's not so little anymore, either."

"So you noticed the way she filled out that bikini?"

He ignored that. "If kids don't learn there are clear limits and consequences for bad behavior, they'll get worse and worse until they're—"

"Totally out of control," Amy finished, a shadow of pain flashing across her narrow face "Her father left

Cheryl," she said quietly. "He gives her zero attention. She's acting out."

"Like you tonight."

She hissed in a deep breath and turned toward the sink.

"What was that all about, Amy?"

"You're hurt," she said as she rustled in a drawer until she found a clean dish towel. She ran water out of her kitchen tap until wisps of steam curled around her. Then she soaked the towel and squeezed soap onto it.

When she crossed the tiny kitchen and came up to him, she touched his face with the warm, wet towel. Carefully her hand smoothed the wayward lock of his hair out of the way. Even more gingerly she washed the skin beneath his eye. Soon because of her gentle care, his eye no longer throbbed. All he felt was a dizzying warmth due to her nearness.

"What's going on Amy?" he asked softly. "With you? Between us?"

Her eyes intense, she gazed up at him. "I told you. There can't be an us."

"I want to know why." He gave her a long look, which she returned. He had the feeling she couldn't stop staring at him any more than he could. She was so damn pretty and hurting so damn much. He was about to take her in his arms when her cell phone bleated.

She started, swallowing a quick, nervous breath. Then she took his hand and pressed it against the wet rag so that he would go on holding it against his brow. He grinned when she bent over to rummage in her purse for her phone. She *did* have a great butt.

"It's Mother," she said, whirling around again and setting the phone on the counter. "I—I can't talk to her now."

"Answer it and tell her that, then."

"I can't."

He grabbed the phone and flipped it open. "Steve Fortune. How are you, Ms. Burke? Yes, I know. She was upset. I'm afraid she can't talk right now, but she'll call you tomorrow. Yes. First thing."

Amy's pale face went as rigid as a stone wall. "You don't have to tell her that."

"Shh," he mouthed, still talking to her mother. "Yes, she's still very upset. Sorry, but I can't talk right now, either." He snapped the phone closed. "Now, what's so hard about that, darlin'?"

"She's not your mother."

"It wouldn't matter if she was."

"You don't know what you're talking about." Amy sucked in a deep breath that made her chest expand and then another that made her breasts stick up pertly.

"Quit looking at me there!" she snapped.

"Don't stick them out, then. Slump or something."

"*Men.* You're like a species from a different planet."

"Mars, I believe, is the latest theory."

Without smiling, she shook her head. "You shouldn't have done that—talked to her, I mean."

"You shouldn't have done a lot of the stuff you've done tonight. Hell, the way you drove, I'm lucky to be standing here getting chewed out for a little ogling and talking on the phone to your mother. Hey, lighten up." He softened his tone. "Isn't a wounded man entitled to a few rewards?"

A heartbeat passed. "Such as?" she said, sucking in a deep breath.

She wet her mouth with her tongue. The scent of her—of woman and violets—drifted to him. She sucked in another breath that pushed her breasts up.

"Don't flirt unless you mean it, darlin'." His tone was low and hoarse now.

When she seemed unable to pull her eyes away from his, he turned her cell phone off and slowly placed it in the center of her palm. "Now we won't have any more unwanted calls from Mom tonight."

Lowering her long lashes, she nodded, her expression anything but demure as she took the cloth from him and soaked it under a stream of warm water from the faucet again. Then she was back, stroking his brow, standing too close to him, stirring every male nerve until he felt wired and fully aroused. A furious pulse began to beat in his neck as he stared down at her golden wavy hair, at her long, graceful neck, at the shapely curve of her shoulders. His gaze lingered on her lips. More than anything he wanted to pull her into his arms.

When she leaned closer to pat his brow, the softness of her breast grazed his chest.

"I think I'd better call a cab." He shuddered.

"You can't go until we're sure you're okay."

"I can't very well stay, either. Not alone like this with you."

"You could have a concussion or something."

"I don't."

"I don't know what got into me. Ever since my birthday, I keep having these weird feelings, like I can't go on, like I'm flying apart inside. Then I met you, which was a mistake because you turned out to be someone I'll be working with closely in the coming months. And yet sometimes I get the crazy feeling…we're meant to be."

"So you feel that, too?"

"On some level. And now I…I'm terrified every time I think about what could have happened to you tonight."

"Then don't think about it." His voice was gravelly, intense. "We're both very much alive," he whispered.

"So what are we going to do about it?" she teased.

Her low voice was so husky, her slanting eyes so provocative, a storm tide of desire surged inside him. Still, somehow he made his voice light. "You're not going to take advantage of me in my weakened condition?"

"Says who? I'm wild, remember?"

"Oh boy, do I ever! But first we need to talk."

She shook her golden head as if bemused. "Later. I have a better idea for now."

"But—"

"I need you, Steve. I need you so much. I'd never needed anybody more than I needed you on my birthday. And there you were. And here you are now, and I need you more than ever. More than that night. I'm scared. So scared. Of what I've done. Of how I feel about you. I think you know that. My feelings keep growing. I can't seem to stop them."

"I said don't flirt unless—"

"Shhhh." Her smile softened her features. "I'm not flirting. I'm real serious, cowboy." She flung her arms around his neck, closed her eyes, pulled his head down to hers and kissed him hard on the lips. "I want you so much." She kissed him again.

When she came up for air several long, wet kisses later and opened her long-lashed eyes, her gaze was so hot and dark, his mouth went dry.

His heart thundered. Feeling wild for her and yet consumed by gentleness and awe, as well, he slowly threaded his fingers through her hair, sifting through the shining strands as if they were more precious than gold. He brought the silken tresses to his lips and breathed in her delicate floral scent.

"I've thought about you all the time ever since I met you," he said, feeling weak and hard at the same time.

"Me, too."

"This is more than sex," he murmured.

"I know." He felt her shaking just as he was.

"It's more than anything I've ever had before," he muttered.

"Me, too."

"I'm afraid it'll seem like a dream tomorrow."

"Me, too," she whispered. "It's scary to start wishing your wonderful dreams might come true."

"It's a whole lot scarier not to."

His hands wound around her waist and slid up her back and then down her spine again, molding her breasts and hips to his lean body until she shuddered, and he felt a whole lot hotter. His head dipped toward hers again. Then his mouth found hers, and instantly his tongue was inside. She kissed him back with unfeigned delight.

He fused her body to his. Slowly his hands moved

down her waist to her hips, which he cupped and shaped against himself. She sighed and gripped him tighter. Then his mouth left hers, and he trailed kisses down her neck to her throat. His head moved lower. Tenderly he kissed each breast through the thin fabric of her halter top. Last he kissed the tiny little *L* tattooed above her left breast.

On a shudder, she drove her fingers into his hair and clasped his head tightly to her breast. Beneath the slippery material of her halter he felt her heart pulsing as fast as his.

"Where's your bedroom?" he muttered savagely as he swung her into his arms.

"Over there." She pointed in the direction of a hallway, and he headed blindly toward it.

"End of the hall," she whispered.

Inside the small dark room moonlight streamed through the windows. He put her down. His breathing grew faster as he watched her trembling hands slide her jacket off.

When she untied her halter top, the red silk slipped from her small, pointed breasts. The sight of her demure tattoo and her dark nipples instantly made his heart race faster. Urgency surged through him like a white-hot current.

He forgot to rip his own clothes off. Striding to her, he folded her in his arms again and began to kiss her throat and her creamy shoulders and then each of her warm, lush breasts, cradling them in his hands.

"You are so beautiful."

"I can't breathe when you kiss me there," she said.

"Your nipples are as hard as little rocks."

"Your fault."

He laughed. "Take off your skirt, darlin'."

A shiver ran through her at his command, but she complied, unzipping the filmy garment. She shimmied and then stepped out of it one leg at a time.

"My turn," he said, his voice sounding husky in the dark as he hooked her bikini panties with his thumbs and slid them down her long legs.

Except for her red high heels, she was naked. She drew a shy, shallow breath and then stood perfectly still as his eyes raked her with the adoration of a man worshiping a naked goddess on a pedestal. Her gleaming beauty in the silvery moonlight was a sensual delight that heated his blood and filled him with awe.

"Your turn," she said in a low, shaky voice as her hands glided lower, down his belly. He caught a breath when her fingers swept inside the waistband of his slacks.

When she hit pay dirt, he gasped. Then quickly he ripped off his shirt. Stripping out of his pants, he gathered her into his arms and carried her to the bed, where he laid her down before covering her with his own hot-as-fire body.

She pushed him back a little, her hands and eyes reveling in his lean, tanned frame as much as he reveled in her soft curves.

Her hair fell away from her face, revealing her darling ears.

"I love your ears," he said, leaning over her and kissing each one of them.

"What? I hate them."

"They make you more adorable. Like my very own real live Tinkerbell."

"My mother wanted to have them pinned when I was a kid, but Daddy wouldn't let her."

"Good."

With splayed fingertips she traced the contours of Steve's muscular arms and ribbed torso, making little circles in the nest of black hair that covered his chest, before her hands drifted around to his back and she pressed herself into him as tightly as she could.

He gasped when she placed her lips against his throat, kissing the pulse beat just beneath his skin. Then their mouths met again and again. He kissed her closed eyelids, held her face in both hands, brushed his lips against her temple.

He'd thought he'd lost her. It amazed him that he could care so much about this woman he'd known for such a short time. But right from the first, she'd touched him deeply.

He caught her to him with increasing urgency. When her hand slid against his shaft, he groaned and positioned himself above her. Then he slid her legs apart. Leaning into her, he buried himself deeply inside her. For a long moment he didn't move, giving her body time to adjust to him.

Her gloved warmth saturated his mind with intense pleasure. If he lost her now, he would almost wish he hadn't been granted this second miracle.

Almost. He would die first before letting her go now.

When he continued to clasp her, she stirred restlessly beneath him and then rose up to meet him.

"Temptress." Chuckling hoarsely, he nipped her bottom lip softly with his teeth. Then, with a deliberately slow rhythm, he began to rock back and forth, taking his time at the end of each stroke to hover and thereby prolong their pleasure.

"Steve. Oh, Steve...." Her fingers clutched his head, her fingernails digging lightly into his scalp.

"Easy, darlin'," he whispered, wanting the heated magic to last. But he couldn't stop her explosion any more than he could stop his own.

Shuddering, he murmured her name and clung to her for an endless moment.

Gradually her fingers eased away. Only when his muscles relaxed and his taut, perspiring body began to cool did he roll off her. She snuggled up to him, and they lay nestled together in the dark, their damp foreheads touching, their breaths mingling, their curled fingers joined. Over her shoulder he made out the red numbers of a large digital clock on her dresser.

"It's close to midnight," he said. "Do you want me to go?"

Her hand slipped down his torso and fisted around his erection. Giggling against his throat, she began to stroke him. "I want you to stay. I want—"

"I think I know what you want," he muttered fiercely, tugging her closer and kissing her on the mouth again.

"I feel insatiable," she purred.

"My kind of woman."

She squeezed him so hard he yelped.

"Do you think I'm bad?"

Instantly aroused again, he ran a finger lightly down

her belly and then inside her. "No, darlin', you're fun. More fun than I've ever had before."

Without another word, he rolled her on top of his body so fast she let out an exuberant little cry when she found herself straddling him. She leaned forward gently, her golden hair brushing his neck, her hands guiding his fully aroused erection between her thighs.

He wanted to hold back. Instead he pushed upward into her with a force he hadn't used the first time, letting her ride him and control him. She closed her eyes as her body began to rise and fall on top of his. He watched her radiant face, loving the wildness that played across it as she moved faster and faster and ground him ever deeper into the soft mattress.

When he exploded, she clung to him, shaking and spent.

"Darlin', it's like you're made for me."

"It's sweet you think so." Folding his hand in hers, she pulled him into a sitting position.

"What next?"

"We shower together. Then we sleep together."

Squeezed into her tiny shower together, he bathed her face. He ran shampoo into her hair and washed it for her.

She sighed as his big hands dug into her scalp and suds ran down her shoulders. "I can't believe we did all that."

"Who says it's over?"

When he was done washing her hair, she took a washcloth and washed his body with warm soap suds until he got so hot and hard again, he had to have her there and then.

Grabbing her, he kissed her hard. She wrapped her legs around his waist and he took her against the slick, wet wall of her shower with the warm water and soap bubbles racing down their bodies. He was shaking violently, and she was kissing him with a completeness that wiped all doubt from his mind until there was nothing but her and the warm water falling over them and the enveloping dark passion into which they both sank ever deeper.

She came violently, screaming, clawing. Afterward he carried her to her bed, her legs still circling his waist, her hair and body dripping wet. They fell down beside each other, covered themselves and slept, wrapped in each other's arms like two exhausted animals after a long, wild run.

When he woke up the next morning, he wanted her again. This time he wanted her to take him in her mouth. But when he reached for her, she was gone.

If it hadn't been for the scent of violets lingering in her honey-colored bedroom, he might have thought last night was a dream.

Then he smelled coffee and heard the clang of pots in her kitchen and realized she hadn't gone after all. He sprang out of bed and began to sing "The Yellow Rose of Texas."

He'd had a lot of false starts when it came to love. He didn't want this to be another one. Remembering her wild driving through the hills of Austin last night, he wondered who had hurt her.

He had to find out. She could have killed them both.

They had a lot to talk about. He had to help her find

a way to forgive herself, because he hoped with all his heart that he could build something wonderful with this very special woman.

Ten

Amy was sipping hot coffee and watering her ivy by the kitchen sink when her bedsprings creaked in the next room. She nearly dropped her watering pot when he started singing "The Yellow Rose of Texas" at the top of his lungs.

When the bedroom door opened, she gulped hot coffee so fast she burned the roof of her mouth. Instinct told her to run.

Very deliberately she set her coffee cup down on the counter and her watering pot in the sink. She took a couple of deep breaths. After she lit a gas burner, she went to the fridge and pulled out a carton of eggs along with some Canadian bacon. She started to make him scrambled eggs.

By the time he strolled down her hall, she told herself she could do this. Then he was in her kitchen, with his dark hair sleep tousled and his white shirt unbuttoned and hanging open. How could she have forgotten how gorgeous he was?

The awesome power of his tall, muscled form sent unwanted quivers through her. She caught her breath, remembering the thrill of being crushed beneath him last night. For a numbed moment she could only stare at his arched brows and his seductive dark eyes. For no reason at all her gaze lingered on the curve of his sensual, kissable mouth. It was all she could do not to fling herself into his arms and kiss the bruises on his brow and underneath his right eye.

So this was how it would be to wake up with him every morning.

Then he moved closer, and she jumped back, scraping at the eggs so violently, bits of scrambled egg flew from the frying pan onto the countertop.

"Oops," he said in that deep, sexy baritone of his. His smile carved deep lines beside his mouth as he leaned forward to kiss her left eyebrow.

She backed out of his reach and tried to calm down. "I'm sorry about your black eye."

"It was worth it," he muttered, his voice grim as if he sensed she was wary of him again.

She felt the heat and energy of his big, bronze body and remembered too well the wanton pleasure she'd found in his arms last night. As he watched her with that keen, male interest, her knees began to feel wobbly.

"I…I fixed you something to eat," she whispered.

"Looks good. Smells good, too." He poured himself

a cup of coffee and sat down at her little table with a view of the pool and limestone mansion.

When she set a plate before him and then backed quickly away, he put his fork down and leaned back in his chair. "Aren't you going to join me?"

"I ate a cup of oatmeal earlier."

"All right, then." A muscle jerked beneath his jaw as he lowered his head and stabbed a hunk of scrambled egg with his fork. "You ready to talk about last night?"

She swallowed.

"You gonna tell me how come you drove like a bat out of hell?"

Making her voice falsely light, she said, "Why does it matter, if I'm not going to do it again?"

He stared at her, and she forced herself to look down at his hard, handsome face and his bare chest. The bruises on the right side of his face really got to her. It was a struggle not to throw herself into his arms and confess everything.

"It matters," he said, his voice low, raspy.

She ran her hands rapidly through her hair. "Sometimes my mother just makes me feel like I'm trapped in a cage and I have to break free. I do wild and crazy things."

"Just don't get in a car when you feel that way."

She tried to smile, but her face felt too stiff.

"You're not a kid anymore," he said.

"You make it sound so easy."

"Sometimes the hardest things are the easiest things."

Again she fought to smile and act as if she felt normal. When she didn't say anything more, he picked up yesterday's paper and snapped it open. His thick brows pulled together. When his whole body went rigid, he leaned over the paper, reading with such frightening intensity she was filled with dread.

Something was wrong. Her heart began to knock. Too late she remembered her mother mentioning something about an article in the paper.

Quietly she slipped behind him and began to read over his broad shoulder. As soon as she saw Lake Mondo mentioned in several bold headlines, her heart began to race.

The lead article was about the body bearing the Fortune birthmark that had washed ashore on Lake Mondo. When she read that the police suspected foul play, she caught her lower lip with her teeth and began to speed-read with a vengeance.

Her mother had tried to warn her at the restaurant. No doubt that was why she'd called. The police made it sound as if Ryan Fortune was refusing to cooperate. They thought he was hiding something, and they were leaning on him.

But the headline that really sickened her was a sidebar story: Oilman's Daughter's Body Stayed Missing Three Weeks. She clenched the back of Steve's chair for support. The story was a rehash of everything that had happened eight years ago. It dealt with Lexie and the subsequent lawsuits against Amy's parents and the charges the Vales had brought against Amy.

When Steve refolded the paper and slammed it on the table, shivers of dread made her feel so weak and shaky her hands became claws on the back of his chair.

When he turned to her, his dark eyes were glacial. "Is this what your mother was talking about?"

"Yes. Now you know. Now you'll hate me."

"Your mother and father were sued?"

Amy crossed her arms and rubbed them vigorously in a vain attempt to warm herself as she managed to back away from him. "Yes."

The legs of his chair scraped the floor as he stood up. "Because of what you did?"

"Yes."

"Because your friend died on that boat? Whose boat was it?" He moved toward her. "Who was driving that boat, Amy?"

There had always been big gaps in her memory about that night. "I…I can't do this." When she backed into the counter, she grabbed the edges for support. "You read the paper. Why do we—"

"Just talk to me."

"What's the point? It's never going away. Never! The Vales thought I should have gone to prison for it."

"But the grand jury disagreed."

She nodded. "You don't want to be involved with someone like me. I'm damaged. I hurt people. I don't mean to. I didn't mean to…kill Lexie." Desperate to escape him, she pushed away from the counter and ran to the window. Her back to him now, she stared down at the tranquil, turquoise pool, wishing she could plunge into deep water and never come up.

"You can't run and hide forever," he said softly. When she heard him set his plate in the sink without rinsing it, she didn't turn around.

She tried to focus on the sunlight sparkling off the pool's glassy surface. "I hid until you showed up."

He crossed the room and joined her at the window. His mouth thinned into a grim line. "Why is that, I wonder?"

"Look, I'm a mess."

"Amy—"

"I'll drive you to your car," she whispered. "I'm glad this happened. I'm glad you know. Now we can end this crazy thing between us that never should have started."

"Damn it to hell! We're not ending anything. Not yet. Not till we talk."

He touched her arm, and she jumped away from him as if he were a snake about to bite her. Her head throbbed painfully.

"No! I can't talk to you! I can't do *us,* either!" she said. "Last night I made a huge mistake by sleeping with you. I thought maybe I could talk to you, but I really can't. This thing is just too big."

"You can go to bed with me but you can't talk to me. Why?"

She chewed her lip and looked out at the glimmering pool again.

"Why?" he repeated. "What the hell's wrong?"

"You read the newspaper. Didn't seeing it all there in black-and-white make you know that I'm this horrible person?"

"You're not. Amy, only newsprint is black-and-white. Real life is all about shades of gray."

"I don't deserve you or anybody else."

"Nobody's perfect. I don't expect—"

"Look, I'm a coward, too. Someday you'll hate me. Maybe not today, but in time. I can't face that."

"So, you'll throw me away along with what we might have had together?"

She felt her lips begin to quiver. "Before we get in too deep."

"Darlin', don't you know I'm already in too deep?" His low drawl softened. "Why don't you give me a chance? What the hell happened eight years ago? Just tell me, damn it. Whatever you have to say can't be worse than what I just read."

When he moved even closer, she wanted to go into his arms so badly. Instead she skittered away from the window.

He stalked her until she reached the door that opened onto the stairs.

"I can't talk about it," she whispered brokenly.

"Don't you know I want to help you get over this?" he murmured.

"You can't. Nobody can. My mother's tried. She sent me to therapy."

"I'm not your mother."

When his fingers closed around her arm, she shrank against the door. Shaking her head, she scrunched her eyes shut.

"I've tried everything. I really have."

Again she was in a boat speeding across dark water, screaming Lexie's name. "Do you know how many nights I've awakened screaming for Lexie? How can I think about you, or having a future with you, when the past refuses to go away?"

"You have to try to make it go away. Not your mother—you! I'll bet it wasn't your idea to seek therapy."

Tightening his grip, he leaned closer, forcing in her an awareness of his large body. She sighed when his nearness consoled her on some deep, primitive level.

"I want to help you," he said, "but I don't know how."

She wanted to yield to him, to sob against his broad chest until all the pain in her heart was washed away. She wanted to be cleansed and new. She really did. For the first time in eight years. But it was as if there were walls inside her, walls she had built day by day, nightmare by nightmare, for eight long years.

"Tell me," he growled. An iron hand crushed her to his chest while his other hand moved up to cup her chin, lifting it, forcing her to meet the midnight darkness of his glittering eyes.

She swallowed a deep breath, hardly believing what she was about to do. "All right. I'll try…because… you've touched me…in ways no one else has been able to since…" She swallowed another breath.

"Just take it slowly," he whispered.

Maybe she would have confessed all her sins, maybe she really would have, if only Cheryl hadn't chosen that exact moment to knock at her door.

"Amy?"

At the sound of Cheryl calling her name, Amy jumped away from him as if she'd been shot. Then her frightened gaze flew to Steve.

"Don't answer it, and she'll go away," he muttered savagely. "This is more important."

Another knock, more impatient than the first, banged against her door.

"But she knows I'm home." Amy stared pleadingly

into his dark eyes. For a long moment the atmosphere felt electrified. Then feeling almost relieved for another excuse not to talk, Amy whirled away from him.

"Cheryl," she squeaked as she opened the door.

"Is this a bad time, sweetie?" Cheryl said.

Amy glanced at Steve, whose face was remote and hard-edged now. "Great time," she whispered.

Low, harsh laughter erupted from Steve's throat.

"Kate says a man threw her boom box in the pool." Cheryl glanced at Steve suspiciously. "Did you see him?"

His frustration obviously acute, Steve flung the door wider. Cheryl's big green eyes got bigger when she saw his bare chest and guessed what it meant.

"Who are you?" she demanded.

"The villain of your little tale," he said in a flat, cold tone. "I threw it in. Your daughter was playing the thing loud enough to wake the dead and she refused to turn it down."

Cheryl's eyes flew from his hard face to Amy's. "Did I interrupt something?"

"You heard Amy. Nothing important." His voice was so harsh and raw it made Amy ache. "I was just trying to save your friend's soul."

"Oh, I see." Cheryl hesitated.

"I'll pay for the damn thing," Steve muttered impatiently.

"Are you crazy?" Cheryl smile was warm. "I came here to thank you." She took his hand. "Kate pushes everybody's buttons and boundaries. I'm sure it was a good lesson for her. By the way, she told me a completely different story."

Steve smiled. "Someday I'd like to hear it."

"A couple of neighbors left messages threatening to call the police. Kate actually called them back and apologized. That was a big step. I owe you big-time." Cheryl shook his hand and then let it go.

She was smiling as Steve closed the door.

"You sure charmed her," Amy said.

"Well, that beats you getting evicted, doesn't it?"

Alone with him again, Amy began to shake.

"I wish you were as easy as she was," he said. "Now, where were we?"

"It's getting late." Dashing from the door to her kitchen, she picked up her cell phone and turned it on. "Oh, gosh." She laughed nervously. "I've got eight messages from Tom alone." She glanced at her watch. "Look, maybe this really isn't a good time to talk."

"Right. Fine," Steve said in a low, brittle tone. "I'll just call a cab and get the hell out of your life."

There was something so final in his voice, she suddenly felt more terrified of losing him than of her demons. "No. I'll drive you to your car."

"Fine."

Without talking to her or looking at her, he buttoned his shirt, stuffed it in his slacks and walked out to her car. She raced after him without even bothering to turn out her lights or lock her door.

When he slid behind the wheel, she handed him her car keys. He drove silently to Lamar Boulevard and headed south. Pease Park off to their right was a flash of emerald green. The morning sky was blue and lovely, and bikers and joggers with their dogs could be seen on the limestone trail that ran through the trees.

"I'm sorry," she said when he turned left and headed toward Congress Avenue. "I need more time."

He didn't take his eyes off the road. "Take all the time you need," he said, but his low voice was indifferent now.

Her pulse jerked painfully. "What's that supposed to mean?"

"It means I wish you well, too."

"I don't want to end this in anger."

Steve's gaze sliced to her. "I'm not mad at you. I'm mad at me. I get carried away sometimes thinking I can solve everybody else's problems. I can't. You're going to have to work this out on your own, darlin'."

He swerved into the parking lot behind his bar and pulled up beside a large black truck. Without a word or a glance toward her, he flung his body out of her car.

She threw her own door open and ran after him.

"Steve?"

His jaw worked convulsively as he punched the remote on his key ring and unlocked the door. When she touched his arm, he stiffened.

"Darlin', you can't have everything your way. You slept with me last night, and now we can't have a simple conversation. That's not much to build on."

She threw herself in his arms and kissed him. At first he resisted, but soon his hand curved along her slender throat, turning her wet, hot face to his. She was sobbing so hard, she was hiccupping.

His mouth left her lips and he gently brushed away her tears. Then Steve tore himself away from her. Pivoting, he turned his broad back to her and pulled his truck door open. When she reached out her hand to stroke his arm, he grabbed her wrist, held it hard and then released it.

"Don't touch me and don't kiss me, understand?" His dark eyes froze her. "I don't want sex if we can't even talk."

"But—"

"For a little while I thought you were maybe the best thing that ever happened to me."

"And now you don't?"

"I didn't say that. You did. You've been hurt. I don't want to say things that will hurt you even more."

"But you're leaving."

"Because it's what you need me to do." He leaned down, tilted her chin up and kissed her nose lightly as if she were a little kid. "Take care of yourself."

She swallowed against the lump in her throat. Only her pride kept her chin erect and her eyes on his.

"You need to find a way to believe in yourself and me a little more, darlin'. I can't do it for you, much as I'd like to."

"Steve—"

"The only way I can help you is to get out of your way."

His face and voice were emotionless as he turned away from her and heaved himself up into his truck.

"Why?" she whispered thickly, stepping back from his big Dodge truck as he backed out of his space and drove away.

She ran to the curb. There she stopped and watched his taillights until they vanished in the morning traffic.

Steve was through with her for good. She felt the

bleak emptiness she'd felt the day they'd buried Lexie. Wrapping her arms around herself, she stayed standing in the parking lot all by herself. She looked up at the big blue sky and then down at the black asphalt.

She hated goodbyes. All her life, ever since she was a small child, she'd hated them. She'd remembered her grandmother coming to visit when she was a little girl and how she'd covered her eyes when she'd waved goodbye because she hadn't been able to bear watching her grandmother go.

A warm breeze stirred wisps of hair against her damp cheeks. For no reason at all she thought of Lexie. Suddenly she was crying again.

She brushed her hair behind her ears. It was going to be a hot, miserable day, she thought.

"This is good. This is what I wanted. There's no place for him in my life."

Yes, it was good. He was out of her life. She could go back to her quiet, controlled life.

At the thought of all the long, lonely years ahead of her, she began to cry uncontrollably.

Eleven

Amy was still crying when she got into her Toyota and buried her face in her hands. All he'd wanted was for her to talk to him.

But she hadn't talked to anybody. Not her parents. Not her therapist. No one. Not for eight years.

After the tragedy and her grief, she'd wanted peace and quiet and control. She'd never wanted to be close to anyone or lose anyone or hurt anyone again. Was that so wrong?

Only, now that he was gone, she didn't feel peaceful, quiet or controlled. She felt so rawly alive her nerves were shattering with pain.

She told herself she had to let him go.

But it was as if they had started a journey together, and now she felt unbearably sad that it was over and she was just herself again. Last night in his arms, she'd felt beautiful and magical and whole.

She didn't deserve him. A long time ago she'd made a mistake that she would never be able to pay for.

With an anguished sigh, she wiped her wet eyes. Then she started her car and headed home so she could dress before she went to work. Except, when she got to her apartment and saw his plate in her sink, she started crying again. The kitchen felt so empty without him. Intending to get dressed, she went to her bedroom, and the sight of the rumpled bed brought fresh tears.

Amy stood in the doorway unable to go inside, trembling, sad, scared. She felt doomed. Suddenly she didn't care about work. She didn't care about anything except Steve. But that didn't make much sense, either, since she'd sent him away.

She turned and ran from her apartment down to the pool, her breaking heart racing in a furor. Not knowing what she intended, she called the office and blurted out that she was too sick to come into work.

"You can't be sick," Nita, her bossy assistant, said. "Tom has called ten times. Nobody can deal with him except you."

"I have a migraine."

"You're never sick. Look, I saw the article. It— I'm sorry. I didn't realize— If there's anything I can—"

Amy hung up on her and raced back up to her apartment for her keys and purse and then back down to her car. As she backed out of her driveway, a black Volvo was heading toward her.

"Mother!" No doubt Tom had called her mother when she hadn't returned his calls.

When her mother pulled up beside her and lowered her window, Amy lowered hers, too.

"I can't talk now," Amy said.

"Tom called. I know you're upset. I know—"

Amy rolled up her window. Waving, she stepped on the gas. Her mother did a U-turn and tried to catch up to her. When Amy lost her at a light, she sped north along Lamar and then cut over to Guadalupe and headed south toward the university. Her thoughts and emotions were a chaotic whirl, but she drove slowly and carefully as she'd promised Steve she would.

What was the matter with her? Why was her carefully controlled life falling apart?

Hours later she still felt as clueless as ever as she drove inside the cemetery gates and followed the familiar, narrow lane that wound through cedar and oak to Lexie's grave.

Much to her surprise, her mother's shiny, black Volvo was parked underneath the shade of a live oak tree with its motor running. It unnerved her that her mother had known where she was going when she hadn't even known herself.

She pulled up behind the Volvo. When she got out, her mother opened the car door, too. Amy stood up straighter and smiled tentatively. Together, without speaking, they walked to Lexie's grave where they stood for several long minutes, still wrapped in silence.

"It's hot." Her mother's throaty voice caught.

"It's Texas."

"I wasn't sure you'd come."

"I didn't know I would."

"Don't let this ruin your whole life, Amy."

"You can't call me all the time and tell me what to do anymore, Mother."

"I knew you were hurting."

"You can't fix my life. I'm not a little kid. You can't buy me a new toy and make things right."

"Okay."

"I may quit my job. I hate it. I know how many strings you pulled to get it for me."

"That's all right."

"I may move out of Cheryl's. I may not. All I know is I have to be me. Not you. Me."

"Okay."

Her mother nodded. "What about Steve?"

"I don't know. I think I love him. But I don't deserve him."

"You're too hard on yourself."

"Mother—"

"I know this because when I was your age I was too hard on myself, too. You and I, we're a lot alike."

Amy read Lexie's name on the stone. "I never really thought so before."

"I was wild, too, when I was young. It's hard growing up. You lash out because you have to. You make a few wrong choices without a clue as to the consequences. I got pregnant when I was just a kid. Fifteen. I was sent away to have the baby. My parents talked me into giving it away. I abandoned my own daughter."

"You mean I have an older sister somewhere?"

Her mother bit her bottom lip and looked up at the blue sky and billowing white clouds. "I felt overwhelming guilt and a crushing sense of loss. I still do. I think about her a lot, especially on her birthday and at Christmas."

"Oh, Mother."

"That was why I was so scared raising you. I didn't want you to make the same mistakes I made. I know I was bossy and overprotective, even overbearing. Sometimes I truly hate myself for being me. I know I call you too much. It's just that I worry. I…"

Her mother's face was so pinched and pale it hurt Amy to look at her.

"Don't worry, Mother. Please don't. I can't believe you were ever wild."

"Why do you think I dress so perfectly and have such a perfect house? It's all show. I was a mess. I still am. Your father picked up all the pieces and put them back together. He still does, and it's not easy. I'm pretty difficult to live with."

"Daddy knows about the baby?"

"That's why he fell in love with me. I was so lost and vulnerable. His love made me stronger. Then I started bossing him around. And he let me…because he understood why control and success and other people's opinions were so important to me. He tried to tell me not to be so bossy with you, though. But I thought I had all the answers. No wonder you rebelled."

"Oh, Mother…" Amy threw herself into her mother's arms. "I'm all mixed up, too."

Her mother gave her a trembling smile and patted her hair. "You'll sort it out."

"You really think so?"

"You didn't kill Lexie. It was an accident. Just like my pregnancy was an accident. I couldn't keep the baby. I was too young. Life goes on, you know. That's the one thing I've learned."

Her mother held her close, and Amy felt a slight lightening of the heavy weight in her heart.

Despite the heat, they clung to each other for a long time. Her mother's hand patted her back the way she had when Amy had been a small child.

"Thank you, Mother. Thank you for telling me about the baby." Amy stared at the trees and vast sky. She'd always wanted a sister. Still, thinking about her faceless sister out there somewhere, whom she would never know, made her feel sad.

"Life goes on, and you can't go back," her mother said. "You just have to make better decisions in the future."

"Steve told me I have to forgive myself."

"You could, you know. What good will it do to keep punishing yourself forever? What good does it do Lexie?"

"I guess I thought I owed her my life."

"You do. But you should live your life. You shouldn't throw it away. Think of all those people in the world who would give anything to have just one more day. Life is very precious. Love is very rare. A man like Steve doesn't come along every day."

It was a sweltering, golden June morning, *sweltering* being the key word. The heat was so fierce and still that even in the shade, Steve's hair and brow dripped with sweat as he strode inside the barn with a couple of bridles. His soaked shirt was plastered to his rib cage. Hell, it wasn't even eight o'clock yet.

The hardest thing Steve had ever done was to drive off and leave Amy outside the Shiny Pony Bar and Grill when she'd looked so lost and forlorn. He'd wanted to stay and do something or say something to make her realize she had to change her life. When he'd left her, he'd hoped she cared enough about him to do something.

Now he was beginning to wonder if he should have stayed. All week he'd been working himself from dawn till dark, hoping he'd be too tired to think or dream about her, hoping like hell he wouldn't weaken and call her.

He couldn't stop thinking about her. Everything triggered bittersweet memories—the scent of violets, even the sight of Noche. Every time the phone rang or somebody drove up to the ranch, he'd race to see who it was, hoping against hope it was her.

Just as he was hanging a bridle on a nail in the tack room, he heard a vehicle outside. His heart seemed to come alive. Instantly the bridle was on the floor, and he was sprinting out of the barn, half crazed with the hope that it might be her.

Truck doors were opening and slamming just as Steve slicked his hair back and slowed his pace so he wouldn't look quite so eager when he rushed around the corner of his house.

"Hey!" Cruz Perez, his rancher friend, held up a brown hand and waved. His pretty, pregnant wife, Savannah, waved at Steve, too.

Savannah. Not Amy.

Savannah was blond, and her eyes were as blue as Amy's.

Steve's heart constricted. Then he saw his horse trailer was hooked to the back of Cruz's truck and realized why they'd come.

He forced a smile. Luke, their five-year-old son, sprang out of the truck and galloped toward him as Cruz, helping his petite wife down from the passenger side, shouted for him to stop running and watch for snakes.

Just the sight of the happy young family, Savannah so blond and pretty and Cruz so dark and rugged, made the pulses in Steve's own body knock with a hard, savage rhythm.

Then Luke hurled himself at Steve, grabbing his knees. The kid threw back his head, making himself as heavy as possible, and clung. In an instant Steve had the boy in his arms and was swinging him onto his broad shoulders. Luke grabbed Steve's hat on the way up and slapped it on his own small head. Naturally, it swallowed the kid, and he had to lift the brim with both hands to peer out.

As Steve held the little boy's jeans-clad legs against his chest, Steve knew what he really wanted—a family of his own. That had been his real dream when he'd bought this place. That was why he'd been fixing it up with such careful attention to detail. Because he wanted to put down real roots and raise his own family here.

A flock of wild turkeys pranced out of the thicket like ballerinas onto a stage.

"Put me down! Put me down!" Luke cried, squirming a little.

"You just got up here, boy!"

"But I want to chase them."

"You won't catch 'em."

"But I can try. Let me down!"

"They've got wings, boy."

Steve lifted Luke to the ground, and the boy raced after the turkeys, which half flew and half ran to escape him.

"Imagine running in this heat." Savannah smiled as she gazed up at Cruz, whose dark eyes were equally tender when he looked down at her. Then Cruz slipped his arm around her and pulled her close.

They looked so in love, so right for each other. Steve didn't need the glint of sunlight in Savannah's golden hair to remind him of Amy. As if caught in a vise, his wide chest felt so tight, it was difficult to breathe.

At thirty-six, he wasn't getting any younger. More than anything, he wanted to bring Amy here and share his life with her.

He loved her. He wanted to wake up beside her every morning for the rest of his life.

Oh, my God. I love her. I really love her. That's why I've felt so damned rotten all week.

If the seven days and nights since he'd seen Amy had crawled by with agonizing slowness, how could he face a bleak future that meant years and years without her? How had he fallen in love so fast, especially when she'd been fighting him every step of the way?

Cruz's voice cut into his thoughts. "Are you going to just stare at my wife with that hungry, lost look in your eyes? Or do you want to give me a hand unhooking your horse trailer?"

Steve felt himself flush. "Sure thing. I'll give you a hand. Sorry, Savannah, I didn't mean to stare."

"You okay?" she whispered, her voice soft and sweet with concern, just like Amy's. "You don't look so good."

"I'm fine. It's just a hot day," he muttered gruffly.

"And it'll get way hotter," Cruz said. "Summertime deep in the heart of Texas."

"Where's Lily?" Steve asked when he opened the screen door of his ranch house two days later and found Ryan alone on his wide porch.

There were dark shadows beneath Ryan's eyes. He looked exhausted.

"She'll be along later," he said evasively. "Hey, I'm sorry I didn't get back to you when you called the other day, Steve." Ryan drained the last of his coffee from a white foam cup. "Got any coffee? I'm out."

"I just made a fresh pot."

Nita, Amy's bossy assistant, had insisted on scheduling a planning session for the Hensley-Robinson Awards Banquet at nine this morning.

"I should've called you back the other day," Ryan said. "But Thunderhawk won't stop hounding me, and I've been hell on wheels to live with lately. Lily and I...we're having problems, too. She's asking all sorts of questions. This morning I yelled at her that she was worse than Thunderhawk. She's so steamed now, she won't speak to me."

"Sorry to hear all that." Steve patted Ryan on the shoulder and stepped back so he could cross the threshold.

"You don't look too good yourself, boy. Something eatin' you, too?" Ryan asked.

Steve jammed his fists in his pockets. "I'll be a whole lot happier when this place is finished."

Ryan stared at him a little too intently. "Right." An awkward silence followed.

"The house is looking great. Really great," Ryan said.

"Yeah, but the closer James gets to finishing, the more he slacks off. You might have noticed he and his men aren't here yet. They didn't show up yesterday or call, or even answer their cell phones until late last night."

"Hey, the A.C. sure feels great."

"Good thing, too. This way." Steve pointed toward the dining room. "When Nita called yesterday to schedule this planning session I actually got my dining room table out of storage and set it up in the dining room."

He'd done that on the off chance that Amy might show up today. Not that he expected her to. Nita, who seemed formidable over the phone, had been handling all Amy's phone calls and meetings ever since the morning Steve had left Amy in that parking lot. Every time he asked Nita about Amy, she clammed up. It was all too obvious Amy had told her assistant not to discuss her with him.

Steve poured Ryan a cup of coffee.

"The gossips in Red Rock are tarring and feathering me," Ryan said. "Now even Lily—"

Clouds of dust outside the window signaled a new arrival.

"Maybe that's her," Steve muttered. "This will blow over. You'll see."

"It'll be a while before I forget those who turned on me."

Steve swallowed guiltily as somebody knocked on the front door. He heard his name. Then his screen door banged, and he heard quick, light footsteps in the hall. The next thing he knew, the scent of violets wafted into the dining room.

"Steve? Oh, hi, Ryan."

Despite her fashionable, gold-rimmed sunglasses, Steve felt the exact moment when her gaze locked on his face. His feet became rooted as his heart began to thud in violent excitement.

"The doorbell didn't work, so I'm afraid I just barged right in."

"That's okay," Steve said tightly.

She was so golden and lovely, such a vision in white in his doorway, she dazzled him. Ryan said something, but Steve didn't quite catch it.

He hated how Amy held him in thrall. How every muscle in his body tensed. His gaze fixed on her pale face and trembling mouth. He wished he could see her eyes, but her sunglasses hid them.

She looked thinner, as if she'd lost weight. Her cheekbones were more prominent. Was she okay? He brushed aside his concern.

Gone were her stuffy professional clothes and old-lady bun. Soft gold waves he longed to plunge his hands into gleamed about her shoulders. A snug white T-shirt clung to her small breasts and tiny waist. Low-slung white jeans hugged her butt and thighs like a second skin. The jeans hung so far down on her hips, they didn't quite meet her T-shirt, so he got an eyeful of too much honey-gold abdomen.

In spite of being thinner, she was sexier than hell today. Had she dressed like that to break his heart all over again?

"Hey, there," Ryan said casually.

Steve held his breath, and his pulse knocked against his ribs.

"Hello, Steve," she said ever so casually, as if their ten-day separation had meant nothing to her.

Steve wanted to grab her, to crush her against his chest. He wanted to push her against the wall and kiss her so much he didn't trust himself to speak.

"Would you like some coffee?" Ryan said, lifting an empty cup.

Amy smiled uncertainly at Steve. "Sure."

Suddenly Steve felt too conflicted to just stand here, pretending he felt nothing when she was dressed like a sex kitten and he was aching to hold her. No way could he sit through this planning session with her dressed like that. He felt close to exploding from tension, when he blurted, "I forgot something in the barn. I'll be right back." Not that he had any intention of coming back anytime soon.

Before she or Ryan could speak, he was slamming out of the screen door onto his front porch. Indeed, he was moving so fast, he hurtled into a heavyset woman who was marching up his stairs with an armful of folders. The older woman lost her footing on the stairs, and her file folders spilled down the steps onto his sidewalk.

As he grabbed her elbow to steady her, a stray breeze flipped the folders open, and papers began to blow across his lawn and down his driveway.

"Now you've done it!" the woman snapped, placing beefy hands on her ample hips as she stared holes through him. She had straight gray hair, a long nose and brown eyes that missed nothing.

"Sorry," he muttered. "Sorry." Then he chased after the papers down the drive.

"I'd run after them myself, but I have a bad knee," the woman called from his shaded porch, sounding cheery now that she had him on task. "I don't think we've met. I'm Nita."

"Steve Fortune," he yelled.

He was hot and breathless and totally out of sorts by the time he'd snatched up each paper and handed them all to Nita, who pursed her thin lips as she dusted off the gritty, dog-eared jumble. "I'll have to refile them all before the meeting."

"I'm really sorry," he said.

"What were you running so fast for?"

Suddenly Amy appeared behind his screen door. "Can we talk?" she whispered.

Steve stiffened. Nita hitched up her chin, her long nose sniffing for mischief.

"Not now, darlin'. Nita's here. She could use some help with the filing."

Nita glowered at him. "I think I can handle this on my own. You tend to your messes, and I'll tend to mine."

"Please, can't we just talk?" Amy pleaded.

"I think that's a reasonable enough request," Nita said when he didn't answer.

Who asked you? Steve scowled at Amy's impertinent assistant. Clearly she was the bullheaded sort who didn't mind stirring the pots of other people's business with that long nose of hers.

"She hasn't been able to eat this whole week—because of you," Nita said.

"Where do you want to talk?" he muttered to Amy, realizing he was beaten.

When Amy's know-it-all champion shot him an encouraging smile, he was tempted to throttle her. "Surely you have an office, young man?"

"In the first outbuilding by the barn," he admitted, striking out across his green lawn and driveway so fast, Amy had to sprint like a deer to catch him.

"How's Noche?" she asked breathlessly when she finally managed to reach him.

"Something tells me that's not what you really want to talk about," he muttered, furious because he cared so much.

"It's called a conversation opener."

"I don't give a damn what it's called. Get to the point." He stomped up the stairs to the porch of his office.

Now that they were in the shade, she pushed her sunglasses up so they were like a headband, holding her shimmering hair back from her face. Despite being thinner, she was as beautiful as an angel, he thought, with the sun gleaming on her golden head. But when her desperate blue eyes clung to his for an unbearable moment, he felt her pain as always. Only, today he hated himself for feeling it.

"You dating anybody yet?" he asked, his voice cold and deliberate so she wouldn't guess how much he cared.

"What if I am?"

He grabbed her right there on the porch in front of Nita and the whole damned world and kissed her hard. At the first touch of his mouth, her lips quivered. At his first taste of her, he sobered.

"Sorry," he said, instantly letting her go, even pushing her away because she affected him so profoundly and he was so afraid he'd lose control again. He wanted her that badly.

"I'm not sorry," she whispered. "Because I love you," she admitted in a torn, low tone. "I...I don't want to, but I do, and I came here today to tell you that. I haven't been able to sleep or eat or think about anything except you."

Steve laughed harshly. "Tell me about it. If you care so damned much, why didn't you call?"

"Because I thought a clean break would be easier."

Nita was staring across the driveway at them, her dark eyes zeroed in on them.

Let her watch, he thought. He didn't give a damn who saw them now. All he could think about was Amy.

"A clean break? What the hell are you talking about? You just said you loved me."

"But that's why I can't date you."

"You never make any sense, darlin'. You drive me crazy."

"If I love you, something terrible will happen. I know it will."

"Like what? What can be worse than what you're doing to me now?"

Her eyes darkened to a luminous shade of midnight blue. "You'll die. Or be hurt...or maybe paralyzed."

He clenched his fist, looked up at the sky and prayed

for patience from whatever god might be tuned in at this exact second.

"Those are realities for everybody who lives in this world. Sooner or later something bad happens to everybody." He paused. "Amy, darlin', that's no reason to stop living. That's the reason to make the most of every moment."

"Simple to say."

"Simple to do, compared to burying us both alive. This house will be my tomb if you refuse to share it with me."

"Share it?"

"I'm asking you to marry me, you little fool," he growled.

"But I could've killed you the other night."

"I'm asking you to marry me anyway," he muttered fiercely, grabbing her arm because she looked so thin and tense and edgy, he figured she'd bolt before he said his piece.

She fought to wrench free of his hand. "Let me go. I came here to tell you I loved you, but that it's over."

"Maybe for you, darlin'—the ice queen of control. But I'm not made of ice. You've put me in hell, and now I'm burning up. You're killing me."

"I've got to go!"

His arms circled her like iron bands, crushing her against the wall of his hard chest. "Run away from this…if you can."

With his hands and body he molded her against him, forcing her to feel the hot thrust of his body as he insinuated himself between her thighs and shoved her against the outer wall of his office.

"Nita's watching," she whispered.

"And loving every second of it probably. I don't give a damn about Nita. I want you, darlin'—forever—with a passion I'm not sure even you can deny. I love you, and you're killing me."

He was trembling now like a hard-run stallion as he held her pinned against the rough limestone wall of the outbuilding. She was shaking, too.

"I've been like the living dead ever since I last saw you, Amy. Is that what you want? To make me miserable?"

She gasped. "N-no."

"Well, that's damn sure what you're doing."

"You'll forget me…in time."

"Not in this lifetime." He snuggled her even tighter against his body, seized a handful of her golden hair and used it to tip her head back so his hard mouth could plunder hers. With a little moan of utter despair, she pushed at his chest with her open hands.

"Don't make this harder than it already is," she pleaded.

"Darlin', quit fighting it so much. Just take one day at time…with me. Marry me, give us a chance, and one day soon, I swear, we'll get you over this and you'll be happy again. You'll look back and see it was only a bump in the road. We'll have children. Maybe a daughter with golden hair like yours. We can name her Lexie. And we'll have grandchildren. We'll grow old together."

She began to sob and writhe in an effort to escape, but the harder she fought him, the more determined he was to break her mysterious resistance. It was as if some wall inside her stubborn mind was stopping her, destroying her, destroying him, too.

"Let me go," she screamed.

"Not till I kiss you goodbye."

"I hate goodbyes."

"So do I. Especially this one, darlin'."

His began the kiss in anger, and she fought him at first. But the instant their mouths touched and they tasted each other, their bodies melted together in fiery exultation.

He threaded his fingers through her hair before burying his lips in the violet-scented silk. How could he kiss her and be furious at the same time? He loved her so much.

His lips were gentle, and she began to weep and cling, her thin face streaked with tears, her slender body quivering, as if she regretted even more than he did the future she wouldn't let them share.

"It'll be okay," he whispered, kissing her swollen mouth and then her salty tears, one by one.

"I must look horrible," she murmured.

"You'll always be beautiful to me." A smile touched his words with bitter sweetness as he kissed the tip of her nose, her lips and her eyelids.

"Don't make us live without this." His voice was hushed, his expression distraught.

When she made no promises, he let his muscular arms fall to his sides, and she began to cry again.

"Lord, don't cry." His frustrated sigh rippled through the silence. He turned away because he was so afraid her harsh sobs would make him snap.

He swallowed a hard lump in his throat. When he turned back to look at her one last time, he thought she'd never looked more beautiful. "Don't drive until you calm down, you hear," he rasped.

"Okay." Her word was punctuated with a strangled hiccup.

He lowered his dark head and raked an unsteady hand through his hair. How the hell could he just stand there and let her go?

When he heard her Toyota start, he looked up and watched her drive away.

She'd condemned him to hell for the rest of his life. He wanted to hate her, but he couldn't. He loved her too much.

Twelve

Steve paced back and forth on his porch with his cell phone clutched tightly in one hand and a bottle of vodka in the other. It was Saturday night. His no-good contractor and his men had quit hours ago. Steve had given the hands the night off, so it was just him and the cows and Noche.

Usually he didn't mind being alone. But he was in such a hellish mood, he couldn't stand his own company. He kept thinking about Amy's thin, pale face and her brilliant, shimmering eyes. Damn it, he was a fool. He'd known better than to even look at a blonde with lost, sad eyes like hers, much less bed her. *Much less fall in love with her.*

He was crazier than a mad dog. He had half a mind to call her and half a mind to collapse in his rocker and drink until he was so plastered he couldn't get up.

Steve debated with himself long and hard before he finally punched in her phone number. When it rang endlessly, his legs turned to jelly as he imagined her standing in her apartment, smiling as she read his name lit up in icy blue on the display of her cell phone.

Then he thought of her with another man and bit the inside of his cheek until he tasted blood. Ever since she'd left him, he'd thought of nothing except her.

And did *she* care?

Sometimes he cared so damn much he almost hated her.

To hell with her!

He snapped the phone shut and grabbed the bottle. When he tipped his head back, intending to slug as much vodka as he could in a single draught, he screamed like a madman instead. Then he ran to the railing and flung the bottle far out onto the driveway, where it broke into a million glittering shards.

To hell with her!

To hell with the ranch!

He'd drive into town. He'd find her. He'd force her. He'd—

What he did, wuss that he was, was to collapse in a heap in his rocking chair and bury his head in his hands.

She'd broken him. Just like Madison had.

Only, this was way worse.

Because this was real love.

Amy stared at Steve's name and number lit up by the brilliant blue display of her phone. Then she clutched the phone and held it against her pounding heart.

Did he have any idea what she was going through?

Any idea at all? She couldn't sleep. She couldn't eat. She couldn't work. She'd gone to her therapist, but she couldn't talk to her, either.

Two things were better in her life, though. The first was her relationship with her mother. Her mother called every day, but now Amy confided in her a little more each time. It was as if she'd always felt a deep need for some real mothering and now she couldn't get enough of it. Her mother would listen and make quiet suggestions, which Amy didn't resent.

Call him. Just call him. Why can't you just try, dear? Like he suggested—one day at a time?

Because I'm too scared, Mother.

The second improvement was that the Vales had forgiven her. Her mother had called her just yesterday and told her Robert Vale had phoned her out of the blue. He'd said that he'd read the articles in the newspapers and he'd realized he'd been wrong to blame Amy for Lexie's death, wrong to sue her mother, that he'd gone a little crazy after Lexie died and was only just now feeling sane again. He'd wanted to know if there was anything he could do for Amy.

"Isn't that something?" her mother had said. "He's forgiven us, forgiven you, for the accident."

Amy hadn't known what to say.

"Don't you think it's time you forgave yourself? Why don't you call Steve, dear?"

Maybe Mother was right, and she was wrong.

Hardly knowing what she did, Amy picked up her cell phone and called Steve.

"Amy?"

Amy registered the profound pain in his deep baritone in that fatal half second before she chickened out and snapped her phone shut.

For a long time after that she just sat frozen on her kitchen chair at her little table, where she'd fed him scrambled eggs weeks ago, and held the phone against her left breast.

The smothering, dark silence of her lonely apartment wrapped her, but for the first time in years, it felt free of ghosts.

"Lexie?" she whispered, just to make sure.

Lexie didn't answer as she had in the past. And no matter how hard Amy tried to conjure a disturbing vision of her friend to punish herself, she couldn't. Nor could she envision Lexie's beautiful white face underwater.

Instead she saw Lexie riding Smoky. This time Steve was beside her, leading both Noche and Smoky through the sun-dappled trees toward Amy, who was sitting on the bench beside his pond.

Lexie dismounted, and Steve took her hand. A strange radiance lit Lexie's face as she walked toward Amy. When she reached her, she folded her in her arms, and they stood together like that for a long moment in an eerie circle of light.

Suddenly Amy grew warm and began weeping hysterically, and she didn't know why. When she quieted, she felt a sense of profound release. The vision dissolved, and still she felt lighter, incredibly lighter, which made no sense. No sense at all.

She got up and stared down at the pool. She was so mixed up. All she knew was that she suddenly felt trapped in her apartment and that she had to get out of here. She wanted to live and be alive. She wanted to be around people.

She called Betsy, but her friend didn't answer. She even called Rasa's cell, but she didn't pick up, either. Everybody but her had a life.

Running down the hall to her bedroom, Amy tugged on a pair of tight jeans and a white halter top. Her black boots with the red embroidered roses stood in a corner, a matched pair again, because Steve had sent Jeff over with her missing boot a few days ago.

After she pulled them on, she brushed her hair and grabbed her car keys. With her hair swinging down her slim back, she eyed herself in the mirror. She looked hot and wild and sassy, just like she had the night she'd met Steve.

It was Saturday night. What kind of woman stayed home on Saturday night?

She couldn't live with Steve or without him, but she couldn't stay in her apartment another second, remembering how they'd made love here, either.

She'd let him go, for his own good. He should thank her. He deserved someone better.

Refusing to dwell on that unhappy thought, she raced down to her Toyota. Not that she had any idea where she was going until she found herself in the parking lot behind the Shiny Pony Bar and Grill.

For a long moment she considered driving somewhere else. She couldn't go in his bar without remembering Steve. Not that she expected him to be here, or that she wanted him to be here.

Maybe she would be able to exorcise him from her heart by creating a new memory in the same place where she'd met him. Feeling more than a little confused, she marched up to the bar, telling herself, Steve or no Steve, a woman had a right to some long-overdue fun.

Jeff smiled his knowing smile when he saw her and said, "Hi, beautiful. Haven't seen you in a while. I like your boots."

"I felt all cooped up."

"You look better. Relaxed."

"Thanks."

Relaxed? What she felt was out of control. That was Steve's fault for making her fall in love with him.

"What'll you have, beautiful?"

"A Flirtita."

"You got it."

Jeff made the drink and winked at her when he set the icy glass in front of her. Then he tore off his apron and disappeared between the double swinging half doors that led into the back, and a new bartender she'd never seen before took over.

"Where's Jeff?" she asked the skinny redheaded guy with the ring in his lip.

"Taking a break."

"For how long?"

"He had a phone call to make."

"Girlfriend?"

"You're mighty curious."

"What I am is thirsty. I'd like another Flirtita."

Rock music throbbed, and she kicked her booted foot in time with the beat.

"You look like you want to dance, cowgirl," a low, male voice whispered in her ear.

She spun on her stool and then frowned because he wasn't Steve. The young blond cowboy pushed his black Stetson back and beamed down at her.

"Sure I do," she said uncertainly.

Even though she danced wildly, and other cowboys asked her as well, her heart wasn't in either the music or being held in strangers' arms.

She realized she'd come here because she wanted Steve. Only Steve. Every cowboy poster made her ache for him. Every horse poster made her think of Noche and how sweet Steve had been over that horse. She wanted Steve to hold her close and sway with her to the music the way he had that first magical night. She wanted to marry him and know that he would take care of her for as long as they lived. Why had she told him no?

A few songs later she started when she glimpsed a tall, dark, broad-shouldered figure in the doorway watching her with the proprietary interest of a large predatory cat about to pounce.

The broad shoulders blurred as Amy continued to stare at him in shocked disbelief. It couldn't possibly be Steve.

Still, her heart began to pound with a fierce excitement, and her legs felt as wobbly as jelly. She began to stumble in her dance partner's arms, unable to find the beat.

Steve. Oh, God, it is Steve. You came.

She wanted to run to him. To throw herself into his

arms. But he looked so dark and coldly forbidding standing there that she was suddenly afraid.

Had he started to hate her as she'd feared? Had Robert Vale forgiven her only for Steve to hate her?

Amy closed her eyes. When she opened them again, Steve loomed over her, mere inches away. His eyes were focused intently on her.

He was dressed all in black. His jeans had razor-sharp creases. His shirt was made of a slippery material that shone in the dark, and he wore a black cowboy hat tipped back at a jaunty angle.

Like characters in a bad play, they stood apart, staring at each other with fixed gazes, their minds groping to remember their lines. Then Steve held up his hand and signaled the band, who stopped playing instantly. After the blasting music, the hushed silence felt even more threatening to her.

"Hey, mister," the young blond cowboy holding her complained so loudly everyone could hear. "We were dancing."

"*Were* being the operative word, son. She's with me now." Steve's voice cracked like thunder.

"Is that so?" her young partner whined, looking at Amy so plaintively she felt sorry for him.

"Maybe," she said with soft regret.

"No maybe about it." Steve grabbed her by the wrist and whipped her into his hard arms.

"Hey, watch it, mister!"

Suddenly the cowboy was surrounded by waiters in white aprons, who gently led him to a corner table and gave him a free beer.

"What the hell do you think you're doing here dancing with strange men?" Steve growled at Amy, ignoring the commotion over the cowboy.

"I don't know." His nearness sent shocking waves of heat and cold through her. "Trying to have a little fun maybe."

Steve's dark head jerked at the words, his gaze narrowing on her face. "Wrong answer, darlin'."

A smile trembled on her lips as she stared at his face. "Looking for you maybe."

"That's better," he muttered, his voice steadier. "Way better."

In the next instant he wrapped her in his arms, and his mouth closed in hungry possession over hers. The tart taste of him, the tangy smell of his musky cologne, his sheer male virility—everything about him swamped her feminine senses. In an instant Amy's needs were as insatiable as his.

"I want you," she whispered, hugging his huge frame, crushing her soft body into his. "Oh, I want you so much. I can't live without you. I...I can't breathe. The last couple of weeks have been hell."

"So, finally you admit it." He laughed so loud, heads turned.

"Don't gloat. Just kiss me, you big lug."

"Anytime. All the time. For the rest of our lives, darlin'."

Her hands twined into his dark hair, and she arched her body into his even before he began kissing her again. She parted her lips, so his tongue could explore.

Oh, how wonderful it was to feel his warm mouth on

hers. And, oh, how quickly her sensual delight turned into impatience. She wanted to be naked and in his bed under him. She wanted it so badly. Still, she couldn't stop kissing him right here in this public place any more than he could stop kissing her.

"Why didn't you answer your damn phone tonight, Amy? Why'd you call and hang up on me?"

"Because you'll die," she whispered. "If you love me, you'll die."

"Someday," he agreed. "We all will. But not because you love me." Gently he traced his mouth across hers again. "You'll kill me faster by not loving me. You know that, don't you?"

She touched his lips with a seductive fingertip and then ran it down the length of his chest.

"Let's go somewhere, darlin'. Everybody's watching us. You're embarrassing me in front of my help again."

"Your place or mine?" she whispered, as eager as he was.

When he lifted her into his arms, everybody, especially Jeff, clapped loudly. People at various tables held up their hands and made the hook-'em-horns signal with both their hands, the longhorns being the mascot of the University of Texas that was a mere half mile away.

"Jeff called me and told me you were here," Steve said.

"I guessed. I'll owe him forever." She blew Jeff a big kiss as she grabbed Steve's black Stetson.

Waving the cowboy hat wildly at Jeff, who began hooting like a coyote, she clamped it on her own head.

* * *

"How many times does that make?" Steve breathed as his tongue caressed her nipple.

Whimpering in response, Amy snuggled closer to him under the sheets and blankets. "Who counts?"

"Everybody counts, darlin'."

"Not me," she whispered, staring at the dark shape of his cowboy hat on the bedpost as his mouth moved to her other nipple and he began to suck. "Counting must be a man thing. All I know is that I'm satiated."

"Ditto," he murmured.

"For the moment," she teased. Wrapped in Steve's arms in the big bed in his hotel room, Amy sighed blissfully as he kissed her breast.

"You know I want you to marry me," he said.

"I was driving the boat the night Lexie died."

He sat up a little and smoothed her hair. "It was an accident."

"I hit that log. We were both thrown out of the boat. She wasn't wearing a life vest, and I was. The horrible part was we searched for her for days."

"Life isn't fair sometimes. I'm sorry. Sorry for Lexie but maybe sorrier for you."

"Her father forgave me. Mother called and told me."

"It's time you let go, too," he murmured.

She climbed on top of him and hugged him fiercely. "I want to. I'll try to."

"Marry me," he said.

"I have no right to be this happy," she answered, her fingers skimming over his furred chest and down his belly.

"Yes, you do."

"I can't believe it…. That I met you. That I feel this much better."

"Believe it," he whispered. "It's way past time. You deserve to be happy. You're a wonderful, caring person, and I love you very very much. You're going to feel better and better."

"I do feel better."

He covered her breasts with his hands, gently cupping them in his palms. "Sometimes pain teaches us more than happiness ever can."

"I was just so afraid to love again. So fearful I'd repeat all my past mistakes and errors of judgment."

"Me, too," he said. "Me, too."

"Until I found you," she said. "Then I lost all control."

"That's what happens when you fall in love," he murmured against her ear as he slid his arms around her.

"It's not that simple."

"You keep saying that. Maybe it is." He kissed her on the mouth. "What do you say we go for number five?"

"Four."

"You said you weren't counting."

"I didn't have to count. I *know*."

"You're not very logical."

"I've got lots of other faults. I don't believe in happy endings," she whispered.

"I don't see this ending any other way, do you? I love you and you love me and I intend to fight damned hard to hold on to you."

"You already have. You made me chase all the demons away."

"It's about time, darlin'." His mouth sank onto hers

with a hungry passion that made wild, joyous music sing in her veins.

For the first time since forever, she realized she might be able to believe that all her girlish dreams of happiness could come true.

Suddenly, in his arms, the world held infinite possibilities. She could even see herself married to him, even see herself as a mother.

Love was like that. It made your life bigger. It filled you with courage to tackle new challenges.

There would be darkness again because life was a journey that carried everybody to dark places. But most of all there would be love.

"Yes, I'll marry you," she whispered, more to herself than to him.

But he heard her and chuckled, gleefully.

"I won." There was a triumphant note in his voice.

"You won. Love won. And I'm glad," she said.

"Are you game to try for five?"

She kissed him instead of arguing about his count.

Epilogue

"I love your family," Amy said. "You've got hand-some brothers. And a beautiful sister. Not to mention really nice parents."

Steve's triplet brothers and his older brother, Jack, along with Jack's wife, Gloria, were standing near the windows of the great room of the Double Crown Ranch ranch house, talking and laughing as they looked out onto the lush courtyard and grounds. Steve could hear his parents and sister telling family jokes in the kitchen.

"Of course they're handsome," Steve said. "Two of them are my triplet clones."

"Not clones. That sounds horrible!"

"Well, the lucky devils look just like me, don't they? Except they're way fatter."

"They are not!"

"Clyde and Miles have double chins."

"They do not!"

"Just testing." Steve winked as he lifted her slim, left hand to his lips, causing the large diamond engagement ring he'd given her to flash. "One thing's for sure. They're not as smart as I am."

"Says who?"

"I found you, didn't I?"

"You are more a bookworm than they are. All those books on the Greeks."

"The clones are illiterate."

"Surely you exaggerate."

"Like all Texans…except when I say I love you. And I do love you, darlin'," he said. "My love's as big as all of Texas."

Rosita Perez came up to them with a round silver tray that held sparkling champagne flutes. Steve lifted two and handed one to Amy. "Thank you, Rosita," he murmured, feeling slightly disturbed when she frowned at him and didn't even seem to hear his greeting.

The vivid white streak in Rosita's hair made her unusually striking. Clearly, she was stewing over something. A palm she'd read maybe? Rosita had the gift of seeing the future. Steve frowned. He certainly hoped she didn't see anything dark in his.

"It was sweet of Ryan and Lily to throw our engagement party," Amy said, unaware of his thoughts about Rosita. "Mother loves being here. She'll tell everybody she knows for days."

If her mother had been overjoyed about the engagement, she'd been even more thrilled when Amy had told her that Ryan Fortune himself was going to give them a small, intimate party to celebrate the event.

"Your mother has talked to Ryan and Lily and the governor nonstop ever since she got here," Steve said.

"Do you think Ryan looks a little tired?" Amy asked, concern in her gentle voice.

He studied Ryan without comment, and as he did he saw Rosita's troubled gaze on her boss, as well.

"Do you think Mother's wearing him out with all her questions?"

"No." Steve didn't mention the fact that every time he saw Ryan he felt more concerned about him.

"It's just that she's so excited about being here. Ryan's so famous, you know. What can I say? She's a lawyer. He's high profile. She's impressed that he's a billionaire."

Ryan's face looked awfully gray, Steve thought. The corners of his mouth were pinched and unsmiling as he pointed to a rather large portrait of Kingston Fortune, who'd founded the ranch. Was worry over the body that had washed up and Gabe Thunderhawk's insinuations making him ill? Or was it something else?

Amy clutched Steve's arm with trembling fingers. "Are you okay?"

Steve took her hand and pressed it reassuringly. The last thing he wanted to mention was the body or his worries about Ryan. This was supposed to be Amy's and his special celebration. Still, he couldn't help noticing that Lily's face was white, and her smile was strained as she watched her husband telling Amy's parents all about the ranch. Ryan's hands shook a little as he pointed to the portrait, stressing the positive elements of its history rather than the negative. He'd definitely lost that robust look he'd had right after he'd married Lily. Was he hiding something?

Hopefully, the body with the Fortune crown birthmark would soon be identified, his shooter jailed and Ryan cleared of all suspicion. Steve didn't like the way the ongoing investigation into that murder was beginning to loom larger in everybody's mind than the Hensley-Robinson Awards Banquet in honor of Ryan.

Suddenly Ryan turned to face the honorees. Slowly he lifted his champagne flute and tapped a silver spoon against it.

"To the happy couple," he said.

"Darlin'," Steve murmured, forgetting his concerns as he held his flute so she could sip out of it while she shared hers with him.

She smiled at him, her blue eyes aglow with the promise of unending love. With her golden hair, pretty face and slim figure, she was so beautiful he felt as if his bursting heart could not be contained inside his chest. He was so proud of her for finding the courage to trust in their love.

Suddenly his joy was so great, he was consumed by his love for her. She was everything.

Carefully he took their flutes and set them down on a low table, so he could take her in his arms.

Then his lips were on hers, and he felt the same swift, hot bolt of recognition and passion he'd felt that first moment when he'd seen her in black spandex in his bar and grill.

Had he loved her even then? He didn't know. Who knew when love started? He only knew that he would always love her.

Always....

Everything you love about romance...
and more!

Please turn the page for Signature Select™
Bonus Features.

Bonus Features:

BONUS FEATURES

Cowboy at Midnight

THE FORTUNE FAMILY

A Family Tree

The Fortunes of Texas are a family who have a legacy of wealth, influence and power.

THE FORTUNE FAMILY
A Family Tree

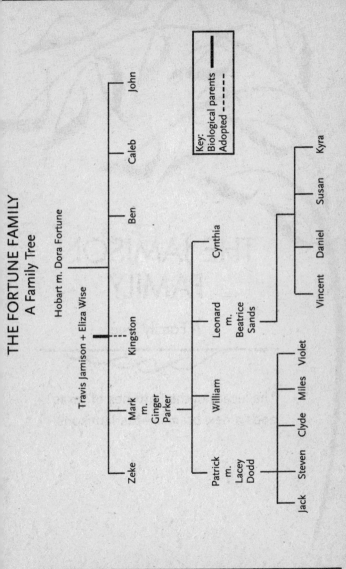

Key:
Biological parents ───
Adopted ─ ─ ─

Hobart m. Dora Fortune

Travis Jamison + Eliza Wise

Zeke — Mark m. Ginger Parker — Kingston — Ben — Caleb — John

William — Leonard m. Beatrice Sands — Cynthia

Patrick m. Lacey Dodd

Jack — Steven — Clyde — Miles — Violet

Vincent — Daniel — Susan — Kyra

THE JAMISON FAMILY

A Family Tree

The legacy of the Fortunes of Texas adds a new branch—the Jamisons.

THE JAMISON FAMILY
A Family Tree

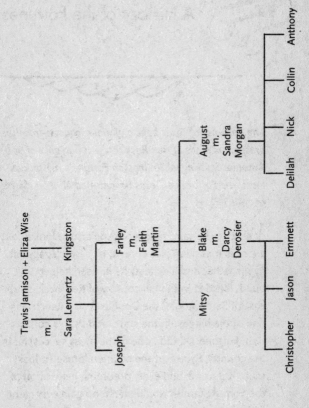

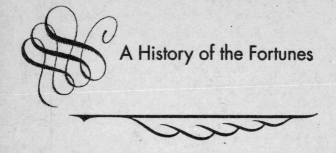

A History of the Fortunes

The Fortunes of Texas have a glorious legacy—from the prosperous lands of Red Rock to the urban glitz of San Antonio. Starting with Kingston Fortune's mysterious birth, the Fortunes of Texas have turned all their efforts to gold.

When billionaire rancher Ryan Fortune looked out over his massive Texas spread, he saw a legacy left by his father and a dynasty he himself helped to build. Nestled in the hill country of Red Rock, southeast of San Antonio, the Double Crown Ranch was one of the biggest in the state, and Ryan's corporation, Fortune TX, Ltd., one of the most successful in the country. Ryan Fortune counted himself a lucky man. But as he, and every preceding generation of the Fortune family, would attest, no gain ever came without loss....

It all started on a crisp October morning in 1918 when Dora and Hobart Fortune discovered a baby on the doorstep of their Iowa farmhouse. Dora knew there was something special about the boy the moment she saw his distinctive birthmark in the shape of a three-pointed crown. Appropriately they named the boy Kingston and raised him as their own son.

Kingston's road to fortune was circuitous. When he was eighteen he left the family hog farm and apprenticed to a mason and builder, Josiah Talbot. Talbot was a religious zealot and cruel taskmaster with but one saving grace—his daughter, Patience. Though pure as the driven snow, she heated Kingston's blood with mere stolen glances, and in only a few months, the couple eloped. Escaping her father's wrath, they fled to St. Louis where they had a son, Teddy. Kingston felt he had everything he'd ever dreamed of—a wife, a home, a healthy child.

Then the draft called him, and while serving overseas during World War II, Kingston lost his wife to viral pneumonia and his son to Josiah Talbot, who took the child and disappeared, sending Kingston into a tailspin of depression.

Limping home, he fulfilled a dying army buddy's last wish and delivered a locket to the man's wife on a cattle ranch in the Texas hill country. Selena Hobbs's inner strength impressed Kingston and they soon married. With his know-how, Kingston increased the size of Selena's ranch tenfold, and soon the Double Crown, as he redubbed it, was an impressive spread. He had the good sense to diversify their holdings and invest their growing wealth in various industries.

All his life Kingston never wondered about his biological parents, secure in the love of Dora and Hobart Fortune. Though over the years there had been many who claimed to have information about his true origins, he never followed any of the leads. One person who repeatedly contacted him was Farley Jamison, an Iowan who claimed to be his half brother—the son of the woman who'd supposedly given birth to Kingston and then abandoned him and Travis Jamison, his purported birth father. But Kingston had used his contacts to investigate Farley and knew of his illegal and immoral dealings in the Midwest. Kingston ignored the man and focused instead on his only true family.

10   Kingston's wife, Selena, gave him three children. While daughter Miranda ran off to seek her own fame and fortune in Hollywood, sons Cameron and Ryan engaged in a sometimes caustic sibling rivalry to gain their father's affections and the run of the ranch. Ryan was a straight arrow and he loved the land, while his brother used charm and wiles to get what he wanted—both with the ranch and with women.

After getting Mary Ellen Lockhart, the daughter of their neighboring rancher, pregnant, Cameron married her. But not until he maliciously pursued—and bedded—his brother's secret love, Lily Redgrove.

From the moment she came to work as a domestic at the Double Crown Ranch, Lily had Ryan Fortune thinking of little else but her; in time they privately planned to wed. But the chaste woman carried the baggage of her poor, drunkard father and reasoned that the Fortunes would never accept her as an equal. Cameron played upon her fears, eventually breaking up the lovers and then stepping in to woo Lily.

When she discovered she was carrying Cameron's child, an ashamed Lily fled the Double Crown and Ryan. Unable to cope, he joined the army and did a tour in Vietnam. While he was there, Mary Ellen's sister Janine wrote to him religiously, and four years later she was there to celebrate his safe return home. They wed shortly thereafter.

Though his two sisters married Fortune brothers, Clint Lockhart still seethed with a secret hatred for Kingston Fortune and all his descendants. Years earlier, the Lockhart ranch had seen hard times, and to stave off bankruptcy the Lockharts had sold out to Kingston, their ranch being taken up into his vast and growing empire. Revenge boiled up like bile in Clint's mouth. He'd bide his time, but ultimately he vowed revenge on the Fortunes.

With both his sons settled, Kingston divided his holdings between them. Ryan took over the ranching while Cameron looked after the outside interests. But Cameron's drinking and womanizing eventually began to erode their investments as well as his marriage. Mary Ellen and their children— Holden, Logan and Eden—stood by him, silent and faithful.

Though Ryan's insides roiled at his brother's behavior, it was nothing compared to the complete turmoil his life was about to endure. Shortly after their fortieth wedding anniversary, first his mother died, then his father, and within a year, his wife, Janine, leaving Ryan with five children to raise—Matthew, Zane, Dallas, and twins Vanessa and Victoria.

Upon the death of her private patient, nurse Sophia Barnes, quickly went from a sympathetic caregiver to a conniving gold-digger. She set her sights on Janine's widower, the bereaved billionaire, and by the following year she became the second Mrs. Ryan Fortune. But Sophia didn't stop at bedding Ryan; she also took up with Cameron Fortune and the bitter Clint Lockhart. For Clint, still consumed by the grudge he'd nursed for almost thirty years, Sophia represented a crucial piece in his game of revenge.

More grief befell the Fortune clan when, shortly thereafter, an inebriated Cameron was killed when he drove his car into a truck. Unbeknownst to his family, he had added a codicil to his will, designed to keep his oldest son, Holden, from living the same philandering lifestyle as his father. In order to receive his inheritance, Holden had to be married to a woman of good repute. Lucinda Brightwater, a committed doctor and Holden's high-school flame, stepped into a marriage of convenience that quickly turned into a love match, saving the former bachelor's inheritance.

After Cameron's death, Ryan was left with sole responsibility for the ranch, the corporation—Fortune TX, Ltd.—and the entire family. Though his children were a comfort, he found himself thinking often of the woman he'd lost so long ago—Lily. When a chance encounter at a charity luncheon brought them together again, showing that their blazing attraction had never dimmed over the years, Ryan mustered the courage to file for divorce from Sophia. But Sophia had grown accustomed to the high life and vowed she wouldn't go down without a fight.

The road to happiness wasn't smooth for Ryan and Lily. She still carried the secret of her son Cole's birth and let Ryan believe Cole was the first of three children she'd borne with her late husband, Chester Cassidy, along with daughters Hannah and Maria.

While Hannah, a wedding planner, was thrilled for her mother, Maria Cassidy didn't share Lily's happiness. Fearing that Ryan was merely back for a second fling with Lily, the young woman hatched an evil plan of her own to make the Fortunes pay. Through devious, complicated measures she succeeded in getting secretly impregnated by Matthew Fortune—via the sperm he'd sold years ago to a California sperm bank while he was in medical school.

Maria surreptitiously descended upon the Double Crown Ranch at the same time that Sophia and

Clint put into motion their plan to bilk the Fortune wealth by kidnapping the son of Ryan's eldest child, Matthew, and his wife, Claudia. Bryan Fortune was to be abducted from the ranch on his christening day. But instead of stealing Bryan, the bungling kidnapper took Maria's infant son, James. Instead of anguish, Maria felt no emotion except elation over what she perceived as a serendipitous opportunity. She merely walked away with Bryan Fortune and replaced into the crib the kidnapper's ransom note demanding $50 million.

Working with Vanessa Fortune, a psychologist, FBI agent Devin Kincaid retrieved the infant and the ransom, but not the kidnappers. Any happiness at finding the baby and each other was short-lived, as the parents claimed that the boy, while definitely a Fortune—due to the crown birthmark—was not Bryan. Through DNA samples, Red Rock's sheriff, Wyatt Greyhawk, determined that Matthew Fortune was indeed the mystery baby's father, throwing his marriage into chaos despite Matthew's assurances of fidelity. He and Claudia took in the child while the investigation continued, temporarily naming him Taylor.

Stress took a toll on everyone. Ryan and Lily once again put their future together on hold, thanks to Sophia's increasingly outrageous settlement demands. And Maria Cassidy spiraled downward into insanity, becoming a crazed recluse in her trailer home in the nearby town of Leather Bucket. A year after the original kidnapping, she sent a ransom note for Bryan Fortune's return, but unstable and paranoid, she was too afraid to collect the millions.

Clint Lockhart, who by now had waited more than three decades for his revenge on the Fortunes, tired of waiting for his cut of Sophia's ever-increasing divorce settlement. His anger erupted in a volcanic display of violence, resulting in Sophia's death. But the conniving miscreant refused to be undone, carefully planting evidence to frame Lily Redgrove Cassidy as the killer.

For Lily, there was only one lawyer to represent her—her son, Cole. With the help of an outstanding private investigator, Annie Jones, Cole set out to find the evidence that would prove his mother's innocence, and in so doing, he found love.

Everyone in Red Rock supported Lily—even Rosita Perez, the Fortunes' longtime housekeeper whose Mexican ancestors blessed her with the gift of second sight. The woman had visions of Sophia's murder but was unable to clearly identify her killer. Nothing could allay Rosita's fears—not even the marriages of her children. Her son Cruz was now settled down with a pregnant wife after Savannah had run away, unsure whether the horse trainer was ready for a family. And Rosita's daughter Maggie helped forge even tighter bonds between the Perezes and their employers by marrying Dallas Fortune.

While bolstering Lily's hope, Ryan had his own troubles. His daughter Victoria was trapped in a coup in the South American country where she worked as a nurse, causing him tense weeks until Quinn McCoy, a fearless soldier of fortune, was able to rescue her. Their engagement lifted Ryan's spirits for a while, as did the arrival of the child of Kingston Fortune's long-lost daughter, Miranda. When she arrived in Red Rock with amnesia, Sheriff Wyatt Greyhawk uncovered Gabrielle Carter's true identity as a Fortune. Through her, Ryan was put in touch with his sister Miranda, whom he hadn't seen since she was a teenager.

Cole and Annie's hard work eventually paid off and he fingered Clint Lockhart. Clint not only confessed to Sophia's murder but to his role in the kidnapping of Bryan Fortune. Shortly after Lily was freed, Cole followed up on a hunch that led him to his sister Maria's remote trailer. There he found the lost Bryan and reunited him with his parents, Matthew and Claudia, who realized their enduring love and took Bryan home to meet his new half brother, Taylor. Maria Cassidy, with Cole's legal representation, pled guilty to all counts and was ordered to serve her time in a mental rehabilitation center.

Happy to be free of the false charges, Lily decided to tell the truth about Cole's parentage. When he heard that Cole was Cameron's illegitimate son, Ryan found it in his heart to forgive Lily; after all, she was the woman he'd loved his entire adult life. They went ahead with their long-awaited wedding on the Double Crown, with the help of Lily's daughter Hannah, who not only designed a perfect affair for the couple but a perfect future for herself with Ryan's lawyer, Parker Malone.

Ryan took his place next to all the happily settled Fortunes, including all his children, even Zane, the confirmed bachelor whom his sisters had endlessly tried to matchmake. Thanks to Vanessa and Victoria's meddling, he found true love with single mother Gwen Hutton, the woman he'd hired to pose as his steady girlfriend.

Cameron's children, too, were all married. Not only were Holden and Lucy and their child celebrating at the wedding, but so were Holden's siblings, Logan and Eden. Logan, the executive VP of Fortune TX, Ltd., hadn't been quite the philanderer his father was, but he'd sowed some wild oats as a young man, one of which resulted in him being the father of a toddler girl. When her mother died and surprisingly left the child to him, Logan was ill equipped to handle her care. As he searched for a nanny, his secretary, Emily Applegate, finally got her chance to show how much she loved Logan from afar by caring for them both. Eden Fortune, too, had been reunited with Ben Ramir, the sheikh with whom she had a son years ago.

Ryan was pleased to welcome all his guests, but the one who surprised him the most was his long-lost brother, Teddy, who as a baby had been stolen away from Kingston so long ago by Josiah Talbot. Now a successful rancher in Australia, Teddy had found the Fortunes when the media covered the story of the successful return of baby Bryan and made reference to legendary rancher Kingston Fortune having lost his infant son, Theodore, so many decades ago. That and the crown birthmark he bore told Teddy he had an even bigger family than his wife and four children.

There was, however, one person who wasn't happily settled—Clint Lockhart. Even after being sentenced to life in prison for Sophia's murder, Clint still craved the sweet taste of vengeance. It was this hunger that led to his escape while getting transferred to another prison. Despite a bullet wound in the leg, he hopped onto a passing freight train and found his way into a trailer outside Leather Bucket. Owner Betsy Keene was so starved for affection that he easily seduced her, convincing her that he'd take her with him when he finally retrieved the money and fake ID he'd had stashed in his old cabin. The gullible Betsy believed that he'd been framed by the Fortunes and agreed that they deserved to be destroyed.

Ryan tried his best to protect his growing family, which now included Teddy's children, Reed and Brody, who'd come from Australia to compare breeding strategies and merge their ranches, and Matilda, who looked forward to freedom from her domineering older brother, Griff, while helping Cruz Perez train horses on his new ranch. As well, the Double Crown was a home away from home for Ryan's godchild Willa Simms. Little did Ryan know, however, that floating inside his safe harbor was Betsy Keene, the seemingly wonderful new maid—and Clint's eyes and ears.

When Matilda was on her honeymoon with new husband Dawson Prescott, Betsy seized the opportunity to win Clint's favor by shooting the woman. But her bullets missed their target and Matilda remained unscathed, prompting Betsy to persuade Clint to adopt another plan—kidnap Willa for ransom. If he couldn't get a Fortune, Clint reasoned, he'd take the next best thing. But the kidnap attempt was thwarted by Griff Fortune, a covert British Intelligence officer who saved Willa but stole her heart. Betsy Keene was arrested but not before she shot and killed Clint, whom she finally figured was an unredeemingly evil man.

With the Fortunes' number one enemy finally put to rest, Ryan looked forward to the future. He turned over the reins of Fortune TX, Ltd. to the capable hands of nephew Logan, who became the new CEO, and Ryan took on the role of adviser. He found more time for charity work, his family and, of course, his wife. He and Lily had been through so much and it had taken so long for their life together to start that Ryan wanted nothing to stop them from enjoying their golden years as a couple.

Some of the family members with whom Ryan enjoyed spending time with were the triplet sons of his cousin Patrick—the son of Kingston's brother Mark who himself had some skeletons best left in his closet. Patrick, a financier, had settled in New York and with his wife raised five children, all of whom visited the Texas ranch in summer. But it was the triplets—Steven, Clyde and Miles—who fell in love with the Lone Star State and went on to buy a sizable ranch, the Flying Aces, which they worked together.

The family had grown so much that Ryan decided now was the time for the reunion that for decades had been planned but each time disrupted. He and the other Fortunes of Texas set a date in May for the first-ever Fortunes Family Reunion. This time they vowed nothing would stop it.

Ryan once again looked out over his sprawling ranch, now bathed in moonlight, and counted his blessings—for health, for wealth and mostly for family. The aging patriarch refused to believe that a family so strong, a dynasty so powerful, would once again be the target of cruel vengeance. Ryan smiled as he hooked an arm around Lily. No, that was all behind them. The future looked as bright as the moon.

On the other side of the Double Crown, Rosita Perez awakened in a cold sweat. In the grip of a flash of second sight, the prescient housekeeper was drawn to the window, to the blazing moon ringed in red. Bloodred... Chills crawled on her wet skin. Her husband, Ruben, might have scoffed at her mysterious power but Rosita felt it in her bones. As much as she wanted to refute it, she knew the inevitable truth. Trouble was coming to the Double Crown and this time nothing could stop it....

Here's a sneak peek...

A BABY CHANGES EVERYTHING

by
Marie Ferrarella

You won't want to miss the continuation of The Fortunes of Texas: Reunion, *a new twelve-book continuity series featuring the powerful Fortune family. Enjoy this excerpt of Marie Ferrarella's* A BABY CHANGES EVERYTHING, *the second book in the series—available July 2005.*

CHAPTER 1

Vanessa Fortune Kincaid threw open the door on the first ring and immediately hugged her dearest friend in the world as the latter began to cross the threshold. Stepping back, Vanessa took a closer look at Savannah Cruz and decided that she didn't like what she saw. Savannah's bright, sunny smile was conspicuously absent.

"Hey, I'd given up on you two," Vanessa said.

Ushering her five-year-old son, Luke, in front of her, Savannah sighed. "You wouldn't be the first one."

Vanessa had dropped down to one knee to give her godson a huge embrace. The boy smelled faintly of raspberry jam and peanut butter, his sandwich of choice. "How's the handsomest man in three states?"

Luke beamed. "Fine, Aunt 'Nessa."

He shoved his hands into the back pockets of his jeans, just like his father.

The boy sat down and immediately began playing with toys that Vanessa had set out for him. She ruffled the boy's jet-black hair, then walked over to Savannah. She took a seat beside her on the wide cream-colored leather sofa. Savannah was completely over to one side, leaning against one upholstered arm as if she intended to use that to help keep her up.

A touch of concern flitted through Vanessa as she sat down. Savannah hadn't sounded quite like herself on the telephone when she'd asked to come over.

Seeing her didn't alter that impression.

Vanessa grew serious. "What did you mean when you said I wouldn't be the first?" She had a pitcher of ice tea standing at the ready on a tray on the coffee table. Without waiting to extend an invitation, she poured a tall glass for Savannah and one for herself. Two bottles of chilled soda waited on Luke's pleasure.

Wrapping her hands around the glass, Savannah shrugged carelessly. It was a subject she'd just as soon dismiss. But she knew better. Vanessa had a way of hanging on to something once she'd gotten her teeth into it.

Savannah took a long sip of the cool liquid before offering a vague answer. "Just me, feeling sorry for myself, that's all."

Vanessa gave her a long, penetrating look. "Want to talk about it?"

"No."

"Yes, you do," Vanessa said firmly. Savannah began to protest, but the words never left her mouth, overruled by Vanessa's deep-seated knowledge of her that had been gleaned over the years. "You wouldn't be here if you didn't. You know I won't leave it alone until you tell me. When you walk in here—" Vanessa gestured around the house with her free hand "—or anywhere near me, you do *not* have the right to remain silent." She leaned her body into her friend's, lowering her voice even though she doubted that Luke could hear. He was too busy playing. "Now, what's wrong?"

Feeling empty, weary beyond her years and lonelier than she could remember being in a very long time, Savannah murmured, "Everything."

Tears suddenly filled her eyes, spilling out. Annoyed, Savannah wiped them away with the back of her hand. "Damn, I still haven't gotten the hang of riding this emotional roller coaster. You'd think that pregnancy the second time around would be easier, not harder." She sighed, feeling as if everything was conspiring against her. But she knew that if only Cruz would love her the way he used to, everything else would fall into place. "There should be a way to put your hormones in cold storage for the duration, get them back after you push out the baby."

Feeling for her, Vanessa put her arm around Savannah's small shoulders. "Have you told Cruz what you're going through?"

Savannah drew back and laughed. The sound had no pleasure in it.

"Cruz?" He was the whole problem, not a solution. Although if he'd only change again… "I'd have to make an appointment to talk to him. And even then he'd probably only break it or, worse, forget to show up altogether."

Vanessa was very quiet for a moment. There was something in Savannah's face that had her heart freezing. She tried to read between the lines and hoped fervently that she was wrong. "My God, there's isn't another woman, is there?"

Another woman, Savannah thought. If only...

"Well," she said slowly, "yes, in a manner of speaking there is another woman."

There might as well have been, for all the time Cruz spent away from the house, Savannah thought. A slight trace of bitterness entered her voice. Who would have thought that the promise of success would do this to them? Money had never meant anything to her. Only love and Cruz had.

"He spends almost all his time with her." She laughed shortly, the last few months crowding together in her brain, awful in their loneliness. "By the time I get him back, he can hardly make conversation, much less act like the man who made my head spin and my pulse race."

Vanessa curled her fingers into her palms, trying to curb the desire to beat on Cruz even though she'd grown up liking him. Until he'd married Savannah, Cruz had worked on her father's ranch, the Double Crown. She and her brothers and sisters had grown up playing with Cruz and his sisters, calling him friend.

Now she was calling him something a whole lot less flattering in her mind.

"Well, who is she?" Vanessa demanded. "Have you tried confronting her?" She put herself in Savannah's shoes. "I know if there was some woman who was trying to get her hooks into Devin, I'd knock her into next Tuesday. What's her name?"

"La Esperanza." Hope, that was what he'd named it. Hope, because that was what it represented to both of them. Hope for a new start, hope for the future. And now it had taken all the hope away from her.

Vanessa stared at her. "The ranch?" she asked incredulously.

"The ranch," Savannah confirmed. "Cruz refers to our ranch as 'she.'" The more she thought about it, the more fitting it seemed. "And La Esperanza is a hell of a lot more competition than any flesh-and-blood woman I ever knew."

At least, if it had been another woman, she'd like to think she'd know how to compete. But the ranch had been her husband's dream ever since she could remember. How could she possibly compete against a dream?

...NOT THE END...

Look for A BABY CHANGES EVERYTHING by Marie Ferrarella, in stores July 2005.

SPOTLIGHT

*"Julie Elizabeth Leto always delivers
sizzling, snappy, edge stories!"*
—New York Times *bestselling author Carly Phillips*

USA TODAY **bestselling author**

Julie Elizabeth Leto

Making Waves

Celebrated erotica author Tessa Dalton
has a reputation for her insatiable
appetite for men—any man. But in
truth, her erotic stories are inspired
by personal fantasies…fantasies that
are suddenly fulfilled when she meets
journalist Colt Granger.

July

**HOT Bonus
Features!**

Author Interview,
Bonus Read
and Romantic Beaches
off the Beaten Path

HARLEQUIN®
Live the emotion™

www.eHarlequin.com   SPMWR

MINISERIES

From *USA TODAY* bestselling author

Marie Ferrarella

Two heartwarming novels from her
miniseries The Bachelors of Blair Memorial

THE BEST MEDICINE

For two E.R. doctors at California's Blair Memorial,
saving lives is about to get personal...and dangerous!

"Ms. Ferrarella creates a charming
love story with engaging characters
and an intriguing storyline."
—*Romantic Times*

Available in July.

**Bonus Features,
including:
Sneak Peek,
Author Interview
and Dreamy Doctors**

Where love comes alive™

Visit Silhouette Books at www.eHarlequin.com   SMTBM

If you enjoyed what you just read,
then we've got an offer you can't resist!

Take 2 bestselling love stories FREE!

Plus get a FREE surprise gift!

Clip this page and mail it to Silhouette Reader Service™

IN U.S.A.	IN CANADA
3010 Walden Ave.	P.O. Box 609
P.O. Box 1867	Fort Erie, Ontario
Buffalo, N.Y. 14240-1867	L2A 5X3

YES! Please send me 2 free Silhouette Desire® novels and my free surprise gift. After receiving them, if I don't wish to receive anymore, I can return the shipping statement marked cancel. If I don't cancel, I will receive 6 brand-new novels every month, before they're available in stores! In the U.S.A., bill me at the bargain price of $3.80 plus 25¢ shipping and handling per book and applicable sales tax, if any*. In Canada, bill me at the bargain price of $4.47 plus 25¢ shipping and handling per book and applicable taxes**. That's the complete price and a savings of at least 10% off the cover prices—what a great deal! I understand that accepting the 2 free books and gift places me under no obligation ever to buy any books. I can always return a shipment and cancel at any time. Even if I never buy another book from Silhouette, the 2 free books and gift are mine to keep forever.

225 SDN DZ9F
326 SDN DZ9G

Name	(PLEASE PRINT)	
Address	Apt.#	
City	State/Prov.	Zip/Postal Code

Not valid to current Silhouette Desire® subscribers.

Want to try two free books from another series?
Call 1-800-873-8635 or visit www.morefreebooks.com.

* Terms and prices subject to change without notice. Sales tax applicable in N.Y.
** Canadian residents will be charged applicable provincial taxes and GST.
  All orders subject to approval. Offer limited to one per household.
  ® are registered trademarks owned and used by the trademark owner and or its licensee.

DES04R   ©2004 Harlequin Enterprises Limited

THE F✦RTUNES OF TEXAS: Reunion

A Baby Changes Everything

by

MARIE FERRARELLA

After five years of commitment, Savannah Perez worried that her marriage to Cruz was doomed. She loved him, but his backbreaking devotion to their new ranch was ruining their relationship. Could Cruz show Savannah that she was everything to him…before it was too late?

On sale July.

Where love comes alive™

Visit Silhouette Books at www.eHarlequin.com   FTRABCER

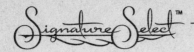

COMING NEXT MONTH

Signature Select Collection
SMOKESCREEN by Doranna Durgin, Meredith Fletcher
and Vicki Hinze
Three women with remarkable abilities. Three explosive situations
that only they can defuse.... Nothing is what it seems in this
action-packed collection starring three sexy, savvy women who use
their unique abilities to save the day.

Signature Select Saga
SEASON OF SHADOWS by Muriel Jensen
Convinced someone is trying to keep his wife's "accidental"
death quiet, former soldier Jack Keaton arrives in Maple Hill,
Massachusetts, determined to uncover the truth. But local reporter
Kay Florio suspects Jack is in town on a mission of revenge...and
decides to "get close" to the sexy widower to find out!

Signature Select Miniseries
THE GUARDIANS by Kay David
An exciting volume containing two full-length novels from
Kay David's bestselling series, *The Guardians*. Join highly skilled
SWAT team members Beck Winters and Lena McKinney as they
find love while serving and protecting Florida's Emerald Coast!

Signature Select Spotlight
THE GENTLEMAN'S CLUB by Joanna Wayne
A murder in New Orleans's French Quarter has attorney
Rachel Powers obsessed with finding the killer. As she probes
deeper, she is shocked to discover that some of the Big Easy's
most respected gentlemen will go to any lengths to satisfy their
darkest sexual desires. Even murder.